In Love with Emilia

An Italian Odyssey

Virginia Gabriella Ferrari

Note for Librarians: a cataloguing record for this
book that includes Dewey Decimal Classification
and US Library of Congress numbers is available
from the National Library of Canada. The
complete cataloguing record can be obtained from
the National Library's online database at:
www.nlc-bnc.ca/amicus/index-e.html
ISBN 1-4120-2780-2
Printed in Victoria, BC, Canada.

TRAFFORD

Offices in Canada, USA, Ireland, UK and Spain
This book was published *on-demand* in cooperation
with Trafford Publishing. On-demand publishing
is a unique process and service of making a book
available for retail sale to the public taking
advantage of on-demand manufacturing and
Internet marketing. On-demand publishing
includes promotions, retail sales, manufacturing,
order fulfilment, accounting and collecting
royalties on behalf of the author.
Books sales in Europe:
Trafford Publishing (UK) Ltd., Enterprise House,
Wistaston Road Business Centre, Wistaston Road,
Crewe, Cheshire CW2 7RP
UNITED KINGDOM
phone 01270 251 396 (local rate 0845 230 9601)
facsimile 01270 254 983; orders.uk@trafford.com
Book sales for North America and international:
Trafford Publishing, 6E–2333 Government St.,
Victoria, BC V8T 4P4 CANADA
phone 250 383 6864 (toll-free 1 888 232 4444)
fax 250 383 6804; email to orders@trafford.com

www.trafford.com/robots/04-0608.html

10 9 8 7 6 5 4 3

Dedicated to

my husband with much love,
who has supported me through many rigorous
chemotherapy treatments.

❊ ❊ ❊

Thanks to Carol Wilson and Nancy Holmes
for their constant help, advice, and encouragement.

Many thanks to Penticton Hospital Oncology,
my second family.

CHAPTER I

The Beginning

The nurse has difficulty accessing a vein today. Poking and pricking unsuccessfully she has to hand over to the other nurse, who, on the second attempt achieves success. A nice back flow of blood appears — we are off and running once again. With veins like hose-pipes this is a rare occurrence but lately my veins have been tying themselves in knots and saying "no thank you".

Chemotherapy is my lifesaver, but it is also the bane of my existence. With metastatic breast cancer, time marches on in chapter form. Protocol determines which medication is administered. As the disease progresses there are periods of "killer chemo", do or die. As the disease recedes and takes a break, life returns to some semblance of normality and the body, mind and soul regenerate. Until the next time! There will be those times in the future but now, as I rest in the comfy Lazy-Boy chemo chair, the quiet beat of the pump infusing my medication lulls me into a semi-meditative state. I can drift off into semi-consciousness, a state which, after much practice, I am now able to achieve. I focus on a particularly beautiful scene or a past happier time, and off I go. This time I am returning to a place I will never forget, to Italy, to the region of Emilia Romagna. I believe my survival is hinged on the fact that I am determined to return to this gorgeous place to replenish my soul. There is a certain valley there, through which curls and slips the Tarodine River. Perched on the hillsides are several little villages amongst which is Rovinaglia. A little rock house nestles within this village and my heart so badly wants to be there.

My mind flows back even further, to my childhood, to a time of innocence and fun. Of our family trips to Europe to visit places where my father had been stationed during World War II and then on to North Africa where he had also been stationed, digging and maintaining water wells with the Royal Engineers. The experiences were amazing for me. My father was not an average tourist. He took us on hot, dusty journeys into the desert to meet the Bedouins, to Azrov to see the wild monkeys, into the bowels of casbahs and marble palaces. He bargained in true Arab style, for yards of cloth, baskets, beautiful inlaid wood tables, and leather sandals. We ate camel meat and sheep's eyeballs. We saw the goat herders whose goats climbed low scraggly trees and munched the leaves. We rode a wild, ratty old camel belonging to a young boy who was walking all alone with his charge in the middle of nowhere, after my father offered him a few coins. My mother and I screamed with laughter and excitement as we took turns hanging on to the moth-eaten animal that could run like the wind. What wonderful experiences! How lucky I was!

Memories of my family's first camping trip to Italy sneak into my mind. A great escape from the miserable English weather was planned. I was unaware then that my first experience of Italy, of Emilia, would capture my heart and soul, and never release them.

My parents decided we would drive through France with the idea of ending up in Italy on the Mediterranean coast. A man of action, my father had everything arranged quickly and we headed off to the airport where the car and camping trailer were loaded into the belly of a very fat airplane. I was so excited as we boarded. My sister and I could not wait for our first "continental" experience. As a child of twelve, to be going to "the Continent" was indeed fashionable. On the last day of school before summer holidays I excitedly told the girls that we were going to "The Continent". I knew they would be impressed!

"Oh, jolly good", they screech, "perhaps we'll see you there. Where are you staying?"

Travelling to "The Continent" also meant you were a cut above the rest. Of course we were not a cut above the rest, we were as poor as bloody church-mice actually, but as my mother would say, "It's what comes out of your mouth that counts darling, not how well off your family is."

We landed in Calais, exited the fat-bellied plane and off we went in a shaky old car pulling an even shakier, more dilapidated old trailer that was home-made by my ever inventive father. It was comprised of wood and canvas, packed to the gills with all the stuff four of us would need to camp through France and onward to Italy in search of sun. The big old army tent took up most space while boxes of rations, packed with all the expertise of an ex-army officer, clothes, camp beds, cooking gear, tin potties, and much more filled every spare inch of space.

Our white, pallid English complexions told the world we were from that place where it always rains. On we trundled, camping here and there, through rain, rain and more rain, soaked to the skin, and plugging holes in the canvas with butter. It rains in France too! Southern France, however, became warmer and sunnier, people were smiling, wearing shorts. Shorts, My God! How alien! I was unable to recall when I last wore shorts. I could actually look up without drowning. And then that gem, that sparkling blue sapphire. Of course if you are one of those who calls Europe "The Continent" then you have to call the Mediterranean "The Med". When you go home and say you went to the Med, the perception will be that your family obviously owns a yacht and moors it there. The parents of the girls you go to school with do have yachts moored in the marinas at Monte Carlo, Nice, Rapallo and Portofino. You do not lie and say you have one but you do not deny it either. They have no idea that you are at the nice school for "Gels" because your Dad got a bank loan, or that you dragged a homemade trailer behind an old car to save on hotel bills, or that you live on a road where your neighbors call everyone "Luv". As a day student, you simply never invite anyone home for the weekend, no matter how much they hate boarding school and beg you to free them from the iron grip of matron.

Finally, we reached the border between France and Italy. Shaking in our shoes under the glaring, accusatory eyes of the border guards who have enough fire power strapped to their gorgeous bodies to bring down a third world regime, my sister and I huddled together. But wait, they have seen the lovely young ladies in the back seat, and so the universal charm of the Italian male clicks in and soon we are giggling and blushing and on our way, quite convinced that we are the most gorgeous females ever to enter this country.

I was overwhelmed at the sight of the Mediterranean Sea, of the variations of color and varieties of the flowers along the Ligurian coastline. I felt as though I had been unzipped and stuffed with bougainvillea and that I might just fly away over the blue, blue water.

The Mediterranean Sea laps and wooshes up to the beaches and rocks of the Region of Liguria. Otherwise known as the Italian Riviera, the Region stretches from the border with France, in a narrow band along the northern coast of the Mediterranean, then south towards Pisa. The beauty of the flowers is overpowering. OOOOhing and AAAhing, we gazed in wonder at the color, cascading torrents of bougain-villea rushing purple, mauve, red, and pink over the rock walls towards the sea. Exotic flowers we had never seen be-fore, in shapes, colors, and smells, beyond belief.

English gardens are renowned for their fresh beauty. We lived amidst a beauteous garden ourselves, green striped lawns edged with borders of pansies, marigolds, mombresia, forget-me-nots, canterbury bells, iris, poppies and daisies. Lavender lining the paths, roses of every color, tea roses, florabunda, climbing roses, a mass of red covering the sum-mer house. Laburnum trees dripping with yellow blooms,

Buddleia, the butterfly tree, covered in fluttering beauties sucking nectar from the purple flowers. A real English country garden lovingly created and nurtured by my parents, and I the "chief weeder", loved to be on my knees poking around in the dirt. I became known as the flower girl because I was responsible for ensuring there were vases of flowers on the tables inside the house on the dining room table, the side board, my father's desk, my mother's dressing table. On the polished surfaces in the sun, when it decided to show its beautiful face, the house always looked and smelled wonderful.

These Mediterranean wonders, however, were an awesome display. And cacti, I had only ever seen them in my mother's hot house. Our front porch was the green house. My mother's territory, the cacti expertly tended, hooky, crabby, spiny things that would leap off the shelves and attack at their pleasure. The incredible blooms, huge pink and white trumpet-shaped tubes, would burst forth to show their beauty for one or two days, gaze out at the world and then shrivel and wilt away, only to make room for another. Succulents with red and pink flowers dripping from their leaves. Now here we were on the Mediterranean coast among similar cacti indigenous to the coastal region, littering the hillsides, tumbling down the craggy ravines to the sea.

As we drove on it became obvious my father was well versed in the ways of this part of the world. He wanted to show us his old haunts, the places that held special memories, the cafes, albergos, old towns and cobbled alleyways, and most important the cheapest and best local places that served gnocchi, his favorite pasta.

We arrived in Bordighera, a typical seaside town, and found a campsite on the pebbly beach. No one cared that there was no sand, we just wanted to leap into the tumbling surf of the blue, blue Mediterranean.

With mighty speed developed after years of training, the troops established camp. Shedding our clothes and donning our swimsuits, we rushed into the wonderful salty waves.

The more they tossed us and threw us around, the more we screamed. Having spent days travelling it was great to escape the madness and mayhem of the Italian roads. A big concrete wall backed the whole length of the beaches behind which rattled the trains that traversed the coast. Beneath the tracks were tunnels, which accessed the beach, just big enough to drive small cars and trailers through. Each camping spot had a big square tubular frame topped with rattan for shade and enough space beside for each family to pitch tents. We had found paradise! The noise outside the wall was sufficiently muffled to be of no consequence. The trains, however, shook us in our shoes and the piercing whistles screeched across our senses. They ripped by frequently but their harshness was often smothered by the big waves washing the shoreline.

The cool evenings were best for exploring. We would walk through the tunnel in the wall and, exiting directly onto the main road take our lives in our hands trying to cross and head up to the old town, most of the streets narrow and steep with thousands of cobbled steps to climb. But oh so worthwhile seeing the wonderful old houses, bakeries smelling delicious, stalls filled with fish, vegetables, fruit, and flowers. The further climb to the piazza and the church, the cafes and bars, the aroma of coffee and pizza. Finally the "piece de resistance" a magnificent view of the sparkling sea and the beautiful hills holding this wonder in their hands.

The evenings were also best for my sister and I. We would dress in our cotton frocks, with stoles draped seductively round our shoulders and across our flat English chests, clicking and clacking our way along the promenade in our wooden high-heeled Italian sandals. I shudder to think what I looked like with skinny, wobbly legs, trying to look sophisticated in my first pair of high-heels. Eyeing the young men who love looking at the girls, I dreamed of what it would be like to live in Italy, surrounded by gorgeous boys.

Italy is a noisy country, there is no doubt about that, and

more so in the busy resort settings. Sometimes we all became irritated after forays into the noisy world dodging traffic and millions of tourists outside the sea wall. After two weeks it was with not too much sadness that our escape from the noise and confusion was planned. The faithful army map case was produced, the route mapped, and I as the navigator, and father as director of all routes, prepared to lead the troops out the next day.

At the crack of dawn it seemed, the forces were mustered. Exercised with the precision only an ex-army officer can deliver, the packing began. The tent came down, bedrolls rolled, camp beds disassembled, trailer perfectly packed. The general, my mother (disguised as the camp cook) cigarette dangling from her mouth prepared a hasty breakfast on the old spirit stove. The bleary-eyed, tangled-haired troops gobbled greedily and given a quick swish in the waves the dishes were tucked in a corner and off we went.

Inland, up to the hills we sped, through the leaning wind swept pines exposing naked sides seaward against the wrath of winter storms and against summer marine winds that sometimes blow off the water. The coastal road was, is, and always will be a nightmare of traffic, but the beauty surpasses all and it is impossible not to swoon at the villas, and the continual drapes of wonderful flowers, and the hairpin bends. We passed a green sign announcing our exit from Liguria signified by a red diagonal line across the name and we came upon Emilia Romagna, region of parmesan cheese and porcini mushrooms, and chestnuts and Parma ham. And so much more to be discovered later in life when as an adult I returned.

As we drove north I had no idea that just "over there beyond those hills" was a little village called Rovinaglia and that years later a connection would present itself in the manner of a handsome young man. This was my first encounter with this lovely part of Italy and the beginning of my love affair with Emilia Romagna, a beautiful region stretched across northern Italy, her calm and tranquil beauty winding its way around my heart. The passion, intensity, craziness, happiness of her people; the overpowering draw and feeling of history surrounding one completely in a cloak of thousands of years, only the surface of which we have scratched. All these emotions were unknown to me then, sweeping me away years later on a magic carpet of discovery. But the seeds were firmly planted.

Why do we love something, someone, a house, a cat, or a person? These are outside shells with arms, legs, a head, a thing that eats and sleeps and walks and talks, or a box with four walls and a roof, or a fluffy ball of fur. We know it is the sum total of all the parts within and without. It is personality, sensitivity, laughter, sadness, understanding, quirks and talents, security and warmth. It is the beauty of the soul. All these emotions were unknown to me then, but the seeds were firmly planted, germinating years later to sweep me away on a magic carpet of discovery.

Emilia Romagna is a region steeped in thousands of years of history, a culture so profound, a people of dignified humility who are proud, elegant and earthy, tenacious, yet with hearts of fire. The tiny villages lure you into their churches and medieval homes, into their hearts. Black clad "Nonas" and ancient old men sit meditatively on their doorsteps, towns and cities are enveloped in old-world charm. Outdoor cafes, cobbled streets with tiny shops, and boulevards lined with boutiques display styles from Europe's famous fashion houses. And the Ferraris are parked wheel-to-wheel with the Fiats, the bicycles with the Bugatis, a place of so many contradictions living hand in hand. The limitless hills are dressed in robes of chestnut forests, terra cotta roofs dotting the landscape tiny breaths of red here and there where old stone houses cling to the hillsides. As far as the eye can see, these beautiful hills wander away on a forever journey. There are mountains and rivers and patchwork plains and fields of scarlet poppies! Blistering sun, howling gales and the renewed freshness of the rain-washed air!

The southern skyline announces Emilia Romagna's rich cousin, Tuscany, the knobby and pointed silhouette of trees like Tuscan war lords advancing. Tuscany calls you to her history, beauty, mystery, her tacky tourist booths and markets with plastic Madonnas, row upon row of little plaster leaning towers, wooden Pinocchio puppets, and selections of ceramic masks. Tuscany has Florence, Pisa, and Sienna with their tourists and hype, with skinny cypress trees marching on to the everlasting beat of the economic drum. With some reluctance, I have to admit to falling prey to the beautiful ceramic masks hanging in every market in this area. I love my collection, the color and facial expressions, the sparkling gaudiness entertain me often. My daughter equates my passion for these gems and my collection equivalent to collecting doilies or crocheted toilet-roll-covers!

❊ ❊ ❊

Emilia Romagna and Tuscany have the same outer beauty of hills and mountains, rivers, of art and architecture, of history stretching back millennia. A genetic bond exists between these cousins, the same blood flows in their veins. The complete area is the birthplace of the Renaissance, a region whose cultural and historical significance has influenced the world, a region that has become a magnet and a Mecca for travelers who flock and gaze in awe at the spectacular architecture, art, and sculptures. These incredible creations were born in brilliant minds and crafted with hands whose talents we can barely comprehend. Here in northern Italy is a beauty and culture that influenced people for centuries past and will for centuries to come. Emilia, however, has a deeply ingrained feeling of sincerity and generosity, of understanding and compassion, rare in the bustling hype of commercialism, but all embracing in this gracious, beautiful part of Italy.

Emilia, how gentle and soft you are. How delightful is your charm. Because Florence was not your child, you rest in the shadows of anonymity and therein lies your special beauty. The imposing castles, cool churches, crumbling frescos, the works of Boticelli, Leonardo, Michelangelo, Corregio, Parmigianino, Giotto, all are here, but they grace the senses with something less ostentatious, perhaps with a desire to remain in the wings behind the flowing extravagance of the rich cousin across those hills. The tourists of Emilia seem less boisterous and rowdy, once they sink into the quiet peacefulness it overcomes them. It is almost impossible to overdose on the culture of Emilia, as it is to do so in Tuscany. Tuscany is a beautiful cousin but I always feel a little sad that many tourists target Tuscany without consideration for other regions in Northern Italy, thereby missing so much of the country's richness and beauty.

Emilia's near perfection is marred somewhat by the autostrada, Italy's super highway structure, roads like knives slicing through the country, the architecture of the huge bridges crossing bottomless canyons may easily vie with the Roman aqueducts. A tunnel vision of madness takes hold of the drivers as they enter the highway. Whatever their regional origin or roots, they appear to become a suicide squad, flying along at 150 kilometers per hour, the lives of all in their hands. If survival is granted that day, the autostrada will eject these lethal weapons and their occupants, where they will go to ground, to the country, the villages, the towns, and once again become human. On occasion it is impossible to avoid this insanity, these screaming, polluting slashes of madness. But beyond the turmoil, peace prevails in the hills and across the plains.

Secondary or country roads offer a completely different perspective of this region, providing a journey into the heart of Emilia Romagna. Walk back into the 12th century, a time when pilgrims who journeyed from London and Canterbury on the via Francigena, on their way to Rome, and then onto the Holy Land, attempting to spread Christianity to the "wicked infidels". Stroll through villages with shady, narrow,

cobbled streets, winding between houses where doors open
directly onto the cobbles, past churches and bars and cafes
set round the piazzas. Venture down the alleyways and discover beautiful secluded gardens surrounded by ancient walls.
It becomes easy to imagine Michelangelo wandering up the
alley towards you. Enter the dark mystery of medieval times
as you peer down tiny, dark alleys where it is so easy to conjure up images of dungeons and torture and misery. The next
corner turned might reveal a bright sunny view past ruined
walls, of a river snaking beneath an ancient bridge and out
across the plain.

A church is nearby, where it has stood for ten centuries. A
church with priceless artifacts created hundreds of years earlier. The doors are always unlocked, the trust of these small
communities is placed in our hands with no thought that anyone might be dishonest enough to steal. The aroma of flowers
and incense permeates the church; sometimes the choir will
be practicing and the beautiful strains of a hymn will echo
throughout the dark cavernous depths of the building. Leaving the church, you may come upon a road leading to a ruined
castle, walls now crumbled, ivy holding together what remains. Inside the ruins, nothing but a blanket of weeds and
brambles covers the traces of a whole way of life of people
long gone. Behind the castle, a vineyard and an old house
reveal themselves. The family is sitting under the trees, drinking their wine. Remnants of those bygone times linger, as in
a chain there is always one more link, the little old lady seated
on an ancient wooden chair outside the door of her house,
the bent and weathered old man making his way slowly across
the cobbles to the piazza. Locked in the moment within the
ancient minds of the locals are memories dimmed with age.
Only a little prompting, a turn of the mental key, and the
stories begin, recalled with clarity almost too remarkable to
believe. More often than not these stories revolve around
two world wars. It is difficult for baby boomers to grasp the
full horror of those events, but in the telling the images are

not hard to picture. This part of Italy was antifascist and had a strong partisan spirit. Men disappeared never to be seen again, villagers were taken to the piazza and stood against the church walls where they were shot. The old people never forget.

The smaller the village the fewer young people live there. There is no infusion of fresh new knowledge, of young ideas. The old people here have little stimulation and tend to dwell on the past.

CHAPTER II

1996

In was in 1996 that we made plans to spend three weeks in Rovinaglia, a group of four villages, Brattesani, Giacopazzi, Casa di Grossi, and Costa Dazi, the village where my husband, Luigi, was born. The trip was prompted by his mother's desire for Luigi to have her house after she died. Her name was Angelina, but we had come to know her as Nona since we produced grandchildren for her. Less than pleasant relationships were brewing among the family. He was keen to be there when decisions were made about Nona's property, and mostly to ensure his ownership of the house.

On our way, amid feelings of excitement and apprehension, we began the twenty-four hour marathon journey from British Columbia in western Canada to Rovinaglia, the tiny group of houses clinging to the windy hillsides that would connect with my heart so deeply. We flew from Vancouver to Amsterdam with what felt like an interminable holdover in the then very smoky Schipol airport. Used to a much cleaner environment in Canada where smoking in most public areas is now forbidden, the atmosphere was thick and disgusting. We were released from this muck as we boarded our flight to Milan. Picking up the rental car we found our way out of the noise and confusion of the airport and to the onramp of the autostrada. Finding a hotel en-route was a passing thought as our second wind kicked in and we flew along the highway. Rovinaglia was so close now! Exiting the highway and threading our way along country roads we pulled into the farmyard by Luigi's sister's house. It was late at night and not a light was to be seen as we stumbled through the village, black as pitch, there were no signs of life. Nothing! Not even a cat! Shutters were closed tightly, doors locked. Oh well, we are hardy Canadians, we will find our way.

We would be staying in Nona's old house, No. 17, Rovinaglia. Meri, Luigi's sister, had explained where the key was. Luigi dug it out, safely wrapped in cobwebs, from behind the old barn door, his hair newly anointed with gray dusty strands of web. As I stepped inside the house, the floor felt different under my feet from our visit years ago when we brought the kids to see their Italian grandma, Nona. Unable to see, feeling round the walls for light switches without success, we fumbled our way through to the bedroom via head banging doorframes built for midgets. Attacked by shin-hacking steel corners we fell onto the old bed. Creaking and groaning, it swallowed us both into the middle of the old mattress. We were overcome by the sharp smell of mothball camphor that some kind soul, probably Meri, had spread generously among the hard, scratchy linen sheets and slept like logs.

At seven o'clock we were awakened from our comas by the church bells. They went on and on! Finally they stopped. We dozed only to be awakened once more by bells, clanging like cannons through our thumping heads. Admitting defeat, I crawled out into a world of woodworm, mouse nests, spider's webs and lizards and scorpions. Picking my way through this livestock and across the centuries-old chestnut floor, I opened the fragile old windows. Pushing open the creaking wooden shutters, I discovered that the "cannon bells" were attached to five beautiful jersey cows, munching and chomping their way through the field. Beyond these lovely creatures lay the fields, trees, hillsides and beauty of Emilia Romagna bathed in the early sun.

Looking eastward, the hills still lay in shadows, silhouettes against the marvelous pale lemon sky, the brilliance of the sun about to explode above hilltops. Fingers of lemon light streaked the ridges caught by the escaping rays. Rich slashes of dark green carved down to the valley bottom where the Tarodine River wends its way, fed by streams tumbling from the hills to the Taro which in turn joins other rivers as they feed the mighty River Po. Italy's longest river, the Po, rises in the Alps from a spring on the slopes of Mt. Monviso, which straddles the French/Italian border. The Po nourishes the fertile plains of Northern Italy from the country's western border with France to the East Coast where it says goodbye to Emilia and embraces the Adriatic with the arms of its huge delta. Gazing out beyond the panes of glass as brittle as winter's first ice on puddles, looking across the valley, I could hardly even hope that this little house might one day be ours.

Visible to the southwest, rising like a golden sentinel in the early sun, was the campanile of the church watching over her charges. The roofs across the valley, some barely visible, still in shadow, were gradually turning to burnt orange as their terra cotta tiles were licked by the sun. I could see the village of Valdena in the valley bottom sliced in half by the road to Tuscany. Life already hurtling through and up and around and up, disappearing into the hillsides and on over the Bratello Pass constructed in Roman times as a major route of communication to central Italy, to the Ligurian coast, and east to the Adriatic. Cars now ascended this pass, the Roman Legions but dust beneath their wheels. These villages are only a tiny part of Emilia Romagna, snuggling on the valley sides where grasslands alternate with forests of oak and chestnut.

Rovinaglia's church, San Pietro, extended and repaired several times in more recent history, was built in the late 16th century on the remains of a chapel burned down by brigands in 1564 during an attack on the hermit who lived there. The villagers hunted down the bandits and one by one they were caught and hanged. In 1580, the church was rebuilt, and it was remodeled several times during the centuries to follow. An inscription on one of the bells indicates the Bell Tower

Virginia Gabriella Ferrari

was built in 1895. When Nona was a little girl, she, and all the school children had to carry one rock from the quarry each day after school to help in the rebuilding of the ruined walls. Giulio, Meri's husband was a bell-ringer in the days when the church had four bells. Now there are only three bells remaining (the priest having sold one) and with modern electronics, the bells are controlled by the priest's computer. He visits the three churches in the area alternately on Sundays to administer mass, having programmed the computer to ring the bells accordingly.

At one time this was a bustling little community, every field producing to sustain life and to provide income, every meadow hosting cows whose milk is the prized ingredient in the world famous parmesan cheese. Chickens ranging everywhere, scratching in the barn yards, rooting through the roses. The schoolhouse filled with children, the osteria cool and dark, a noisy smoky place where the old men sat drinking wine and solving the problems of their insular world. Sixty or seventy families once lived here. Now just a few permanent residents remain, the hardy souls born and bred to die here.

❈ ❈ ❈

To claim Luigi's heritage we had to decide how to proceed without offending family members, treading on no toes. Being usurpers, those long absent visitors from Canada, I was apprehensive about how we would be received. What rights did we have? We had not scratched a living out of the land, we had not worn our fingers and bodies to the bone, slaving to maintain the livestock, the farm. Our only contribution had been financial aid for Nona. Perhaps her bequest of No. 17, Rovinaglia to Luigi showed her gratitude, but I could not shake the feeling of appearing like grabbing foreigners, fighting for the spoils.

When Luigi's father, Lorenzo, died in 1974, the legacy of

his father's house in San Vincenzo, a village below Rovinaglia on the hillside, was a problem more than anything else. Living and settled in Canada, as a young man raising a family, Luigi really had no desire at that time to renew ties with the old country. His nephew, Stefano, (Meri and Giulio's second son) had recently married. Living with his new wife Anna in the same house as Meri was difficult at times. The solution was simple, give them Lorenzo's old house. They could leave the cloying paranoia of Rovinaglia and set up home in the happier environment of San Vincenzo.

Older and wiser now, Luigi can see the merits of having a little place in Italy. This time he wanted his little bit of Rovinaglia, and when I opened those creaking old shutters, I wanted it also.

My memories of our first visit years ago with the kids were very vivid and I recall poking around in a room at the end of Nona's house, looking at old furniture and clothes hanging on nails, boxes full of ancient linen, and old photographs. I was amazed to find an earth wall behind an old curtain hanging on a sagging wire. The ceilings were black with grime, an accumulation of soot and smoke from fires lit thousands of times over the years since Grandpa Luigi had built the little house. The kitchen floor was also earth, compacted by years of treading feet. A single naked twenty-five watt bulb hung on a wriggley old wire from a beam and did little to brighten the gloom. The kitchen was the only warm room in the house. The wood stove also designed for cooking, standing in the middle, allowed space to do not much more than sit on the old bench or on one of the two chairs at the little wooden table. Set in the rock wall was a china cabinet fronted by two old, painted and peeling glass windows that must have been from another old house. They protected mementos and years of memories of an old lady. Faded brown photographs posed so perfectly by serious family members attired in their best Sunday dress. Colored pictures, hand tinted, of Madonnas from different feasts, and churches. An array of aperitif glasses, not one matching, little espresso cups, and a bright red plastic holder for a glass, standing empty, and totally incongruous among its companions like a rooster strutting among his dowdy hens. There were two chipped and cracked small plates set upright against the gaudy backdrop. Madonnas smiling peacefully, cradling their own baby Jesuses. A display of memories of Nona's life set against a background of brittle, crinkled kitchen paper of several different designs and colors, rusty nails holding it to the rocks and mortar behind. The three rooms she used at that time were the kitchen, with access through a small barn-style door to a bedroom about the same size as the kitchen. Beyond the bedroom and through an opening in the meter thick wall was a smaller room containing a rusty old Victorian bed and a steamer trunk. The bedroom was filled almost to bursting with a monstrous old bed with wooden head and foot boards and a sagging old spring and mattress. There was no bathroom. A little outhouse stood beneath a drooping old lean-to. We drew water from the village tap, washed the kids in the old tin bath, and experienced life in the raw.

While we were there, Nona insisted that we use her bed and that we put the kids in the small room. Our insistence that she use her own bed only served to strengthen her resolve not to. She spent fourteen nights on the old wooden pew-like bench in the kitchen, a fixture of every older cottage and even some newer homes. She spread a few thin old pillows to cushion her rheumatic joints against the old chestnut wood, two relics together.

I remember how the dreary atmosphere in the kitchen urged me into the fresh, bright outdoors. I remember walking round the end of the house and noticing the climbing pink rose snaking its way up the rock wall beside the old cantina. On the eastern side of the house facing the valley was a wonderful hedge of aromatic Syringa and two beautiful fig trees from which, years later, I would be able to pick white and black figs. Oh so good. Back up behind the house ran a bumpy cobbled and weedy lane, where one might almost reach up and touch the eaves.

The dry rock construction of the cottage was wonderful. I was amazed at the precision with which the rocks were placed, so perfectly at right angles with each other, the corner stones just immense. Over the door opening from the kitchen into the back lane was a rock engraved with the year 1883 and the name of Nona's father, Luigi Dora. Natural slabs of flat rock, pianelli di sasso, gathered from the banks of the river and the hillsides, formed the roof, the successive layers secured only by their weight. Rising from the roof was an old slate chimney, a small square tower with openings on each side and a flat top-slate.

All these years later, the rocks are covered with ugly gray cement stucco. The wonderful rock over the old door is also covered. There is now, however, a lovely terra cotta roof. The new chimney stands gaily on guard with a jaunty little domed hat decorated with a terracotta pompom. A new and fresh interior, a tiled kitchen floor, and a bathroom with the biggest bath I had ever seen greeted us. Some of the old things remained. The old beds, table and chairs, the kitchen sink and the china cabinet hosting a few of the old mementos, now accompanied by colored photographs of grandchildren and more religious paraphernalia. The red plastic mug holder still stands cheekily among its ancient mates. Above the new steel kitchen door with the barred window hangs Jesus on his cross, a little plastic dead man overseeing all who enter this house.

During the next couple of days, we rearranged the rooms to suit our lifestyle a little better. The area at the end of the house is now a large empty room, the earth wall is now covered by a rock wall. I wished it had been bare rock but it was covered in stucco. We took the impossibly huge bed to pieces and dragged it and an old wardrobe into this end room and created a bedroom for ourselves. The ancient Victorian iron bedstead remained in the small room, it and most of the floor covered with junk, old farm chairs, a bed spring, boxes, suitcases full of old curtains and clothes, wood-wormy side tables, several pictures of different Madonnas, and boxes of old linen. We transformed what had been the original bedroom off the kitchen into a dining and sitting room by dragging the old bench in and the tiny kitchen table. With the early sunlight streaming in and fresh flowers on the table and windowsill, the room was lovely.

I think we were actually keeping as busy as possible as a way of warding off the inevitability of family discussions over Nona's properties. I almost felt as though we were at "The Last Supper" the night before the family meeting, trying to stuff down the meal, my stomach churning continuously. Thinking why on earth should I feel so nervous? Luigi is perfectly capable of standing his ground in a firm and gentlemanly manner.

Meri had gained a reputation over the years of being stubborn, hard, and insistent. I do not know where or when the reputation of this woman's fearless personality had been born. I suppose, over the years, I had heard family gossip via Luigi about her stubbornness, her desire to control the family. My own memories of her, from our visit twenty-five years ago, were of a skinny little woman, very kind, mostly happy, with a mouthful of black, rotten stumpy teeth, and hairy legs. She worked continuously, cooking, or in the farmyard, up every morning at five o'clock to milk the cows, then to herd them down to the field, then bringing them back to the barn again for the four o'clock milking. Perhaps the death of her mother had required that she, by tradition, should step into those matriarchal shoes. All I know is that I was expecting the "Iron Maiden" herself, but was not sure why.

The following morning we took the bit between our teeth and began the walk to Meri's house. My tough Canadian boldness began to desert me and trembling with fear at the thought of the ensuing face-off, I walked close at Luigi's heels like a sniveling puppy. In the face of battle, my true colors were revealed. I tried to conjure up the bravery of Sgt. James Leary, my great-great grandfather riding with the six hundred into the "Valley of Death" with the Light Brigade. He survived — so would I!

My apprehension of what was to come made the three-minute walk seem endless. We walked up the short narrow cobbled lane between Nona's house and the monstrous ugly grey house owned by a man who visits each summer. Later I nicknamed him the "Land Baron" because, from his conversations, he appears to own everything and everywhere. Continuing on, we passed Pepino and Lina's house, which is attached to Nona's cottage. Pepino is Luigi's godfather, a delightful, tall, almost regal looking elderly man who really enjoys our conversations, appreciating what we have to relate as opposed to jumping in with his next thought like a lot of old folks do. Between his house and the next, Marietta's, is a steep footpath down to the gardens and fields beyond or on along the eastside of Meri's house, which ends the chain of houses. This day, however, we took the back lane coming out into the gravel and paved farmyard round to the front of

Meri's big house. Painted a lovely buttery-melony yellow with green shutters, the house shone like a ray of sun from among the ugly, gray cemented walls of its companions.

We walked on across the farm yard and noticed that Giulio was in his garage snoring away with Bianca the one-and-a-half-eared cat on his chest. Various types of farm equipment are parked in the big barn with his old jeep and a tiny Fiat squeezed in beside them. The story of Bianca and her one-and-a-half ears is quite amusing and unbelievable to me. Apparently she was taken to the vet to be spayed (which I find totally incredible because all the cats are constantly producing litters), and came back with one of her ears minus one-half inch cut from the top. Meri says that was done to signify Bianca's sterility. Must be the only sterile cat in Italy!

The view once round the corner was wonderful. Framed between Meri's house and the two old rock cottages attached to the big barn was the village of Brattesani, its red roofs falling away down the hillside, a beautiful backdrop for the "Iron Maiden" who now stood before us. Meri, certainly much older, but with lovely white teeth, a frothy gray curly hairdo, and whiskers to match, a bit of extra fat on her once lean body. She had transformed from the ogre I expected into a small, smiling person with floured hands, and with arms outstretched in welcome. She wore old leather ankle boots and woolly socks with the usual pinafore over a knee-length straight black skirt.

We did the cheek-to-cheek thing and went inside. On the right was Pierina's "Dungeon". Pierina is Giulio's sister. Her life is spent in her one room downstairs, with her bedroom upstairs, and she tramps out to her outhouse as she refuses to use Meri's bathroom. A long flight of wide marble stairs lead up to the second floor bedrooms. We entered the very warm kitchen that also serves as a dining and living room where the family spends most of their time when home. A very fancy dining room down the hall awaits its Epiphany and Easter guests. As we sat on the wooden bench, Meri and

Luigi chatting away while she rolled her pasta, Giulio, and Roberto, her oldest son, arrived and sat at the table. The ever-present television was talking to itself, up on the corner of the sideboard.

The family discussion now taking place seemed civilized and pleasant. Was I wrong in my opinion of Meri after all? My guard down, I was shaken when Meri's voice rose, and then Roberto and Giulio and finally Luigi. This is common in Italian families, all speaking at once trying to be heard. The noise eventually reaches a crescendo. A moment of quiet bathes the room in peace, and then off they go again. The conversations and shouting matches always sound like arguments but usually they are the result of over zealousness and excitement; however, this family discussion had turned into a free for all. Not understanding a word, I quietly exited to the farmyard and to the peace and tranquility of Nona's house.

The family discussions, the ensuing meetings, were at times amusing, frustrating, arduous and just plain ridiculous. This formidable woman obviously headed up the family and was certainly a force to be dealt with. A quiet, unassuming, delightful husband, Giulio, and four children, Roberto, Stefano, Georgio, and Giuliana, on whose behalf she fought tooth and nail for their shares of every piece of woodland, fields and meadows, barns and footpaths. One might say of course, that Meri and her family had every right, having worked their fingers to the bone on the land. This woman ruled the roost and cracked the whip. Her husband, sons, even cousins, uncles, aunts and neighbors jumped accordingly, except for Giuliana, her daughter who refused to be corralled. Were the genes of stubbornness coming through already? Oh this woman Meri, was huge and fearful running round the farmyard whacking at the skinny cats with a broomstick, stomping on scorpions and decapitating the snakes. Someone to be wary of for sure. Five feet two and one hundred and ten pounds in no way diminished the clout she carried. Her aggressive stance made about as much impression on Luigi, however, as water on a duck's back. We just do not operate this way at home. Confrontation is not a part of our lives and we float along calmly instead of rushing through what seem like death defying rapids.

Further discussions took place in Giulio's garage, an old place across the yard from the house, a place of disarray and dust, packed with years of junk. A calendar, frozen in time ten years before at the month of July, 1985, hanging on the wall seeming to point out that time here was almost at a stand-still. There is an old wooden bench like a church pew, with flat, worn cushions on which Giulio would stretch out, snuggled on his chest the cat, safe for the minute from the old harridan with the broom. This sacred site, this sanctuary of one old man, was invaded for the family meetings. He was regularly turfed off his old bench and told to sit up and make room for the "members of the board", and once again we met for negotiations. The cat was long since gone having heard Meri's voice advancing. The "Board" consisted of "Madam Chairwoman" Meri, Roberto her eldest son, Giulio, and Luigi. Curiosity prompted others to arrive; cousin Bruno who lived in a separate house across from Meri's, Pierina, Giulio's sis-ter, and one of Giulio's brothers, none of these people having anything to do with the affair. Everybody talked at once, some intermittently giving me the evil eye as though I should not be there, but neither should you, I thought. Every surface occupied by a bottom! I almost expected the priest to pop in, he would have the hot seat, the stove being the only free sur-face remaining.

Negotiations were becoming acrimonious. There was no arbitrator, what was the point? The mother hen ruled the roost and would continue to do so. Luigi did his best to trans-late, but he was soon speaking Italian to me and English to his family. Such confusion! Papers were produced, diagrams of land outlined in different colors. We were yellow, Meri's was red—too much red I thought, not enough yellow, my favorite color. Someone, I wondered who, had already made

decisions about who would have what. I could see Luigi looking annoyed. He raised his voice above the others and those
with no personal claim were dismissed unceremoniously,
which left a manageable group of four. I stuck out like a sore
thumb and attempted to hide away in the corner among the
potatoes. The diagram indicated that Luigi's plots were too
far away, steep slopes and gullies. Still nothing was indicated
regarding Nona's house. But now we were getting down to
brass tacks—the real dealing was starting. Luigi named his
choices, Genovese, Banshoele, and fields near the house.

"No," said Meri "you can't have those. I promised them to
Roberto. You can have the forest up past Monte Pero."

"What good will that do me?" he countered. "It's miles away.
I want land near the village, close to the house."

"Well," said Meri, her cheeks flushed from the heat of the
stove, "perhaps you can have the hillside where the family
used to grow grapes. That's close by."

"I want that and two other pieces", he said.

She nixed that also. All this was going nowhere. Then
Roberto, the peacemaker, stood. Suggesting the meeting shut
up shop for the day, he left. Without one of the major players
there was no point in continuing. I started babbling on about
the gorgeous weather and the dogs outside but I may as well
not have been there. Meri stomped off to her kitchen, Giulio
lay back on his bench and closed his eyes. The television continued to blab on, and we left. There was somewhere nicer to
be. We headed for Nona's house.

These meetings punctuated our stay. Would there ever be
resolution? I just placated my heart by hoping and praying
that we would eventually get the pieces of land we wanted. I
hoped that all the bargaining and fighting would one day
come to an end, that we would all live amicably and that
Luigi and I would own Banshoele and Genovese, our favorite parcels and of course Nona's house. Some pieces of land
have nicknames the reasons for which are often lost in history. Luigi loved Banshoele. Taking the scythe and clippers

and other tools, he could disappear into its jungle a kilometer or so from the house, away from the prying eyes of the
villagers who have a penchant for wanting to know everything about everything. I love Genovese. Genovese literally
means "People from Genoa". It sits on the western side of
the hill as opposed to the eastern slope to which Rovinaglia
clings. It is protected from the wind, sloping gently at first
towards the tinkling creek that winds its way down to the
Taro then more steeply, overgrown with brambles, wild roses
and canopied with hundreds of chestnut trees. At points the
River Taro is visible as it snakes through the valley, city rooftops and bridges also peek through. My dream would be to
build a little rock house with a red tiled roof, snuggled at the
top of Genovese, a stand of chestnut trees behind, and beyond those stretching back up the hill the beautiful wild flower
meadows, an ancient oak perfectly positioned to shade the
front porch. It could be my little place where the wind cannot reach me, where silence is broken only by the birds or by
a distant tractor, but mostly, where I would not be affected
by the petty, narrow minds and the ever-watchful eye of
mother hen and the other inquisitive villagers.

Sometimes we would walk over to Genovese in the evening
to watch the sunsets streaking the sky in fiery blazes across
the distant mountains, the slashes of indigo clouds, the butter background turning to lemon. It was not hard to stay
silent in the presence of these awesome natural wonders.

Dotting the opposite hillsides are many little houses and
villages. The most beautiful of these is Compiano, my favorite, topped by the castle, construction of which began in the
year 852. This village is home to many artists and artisans. A
wealth of beauty and history is hidden away in the cool
cobbled streets and alleyways. No cars are allowed within
the walls except for those of the residents, and so this beauty
remains fresh and clean. Behind thick studded, centuries-
old doors, the potters and painters, the sculptors and
craftsmen create from their hearts. The castle has been host

to many different aristocratic families: Costello, Malaspina, Landi, Visconte, Piccanino, Farnese, Borbonni, the list is formidable. More recently it was a school for young ladies. The last owner was a countess who remodeled the inside, draping the walls with heavy velvets and silks completely at odds with the castle's design. She left her Irish wolfhound and the castle to the community. We saw the dog a few times enclosed in a pen with a rock kennel. The poor thing had no one to socialize with, only the keeper of the castle who was responsible for the dogs daily care and feeding. The castle is now a museum exhibiting artifacts from different eras. These artifacts do not display well within the heavy Victorian décor. The castle is, however, imposing and stands guard over the village with its rock wall splendor sprouting turrets and gargoyles and glorious marble statues.

On the eastern side of the hill overlooking Rovinaglia there is a particular meadow, my favorite, where I like to walk and sit, contemplate and draw. The aroma of the wild flowers, scabious, borage, buttercups, fennel, mallow, cornflowers, clover, is wonderful. So many colors, too beautiful, set in a carpet of green, stretching away down the hillsides leading my eyes to the red roofs surrounding the church in Rovinaglia and then across the valley to Valdena with its own ever-watchful church. Each village is a nucleus of beings, tiny pieces of a huge and wonderful puzzle. Drawing in the feelings and beauty of this meadow, of the views up and down the valley, is a wonderful way to forget the family in-fighting, the spats and squabbles. I wish Luigi would spend more time up here in the peace and solitude, to renew his spirit when it is low. I see a subtle change in him, very slight but evident in the occasional paranoid remark he makes. Will he become one of the negative, complaining, old men of the village?

PRIEST'S WINDOW   V FERRARI

It is Sunday. The computerized church bell is tolling, call-ing the faithful to church. Rovinaglia's bells are the third to ring, taking their turn according to the priests schedule, the priest who sold the kid's soccer field and one of the church bells, the same priest who sits outside his church holding court in the other village below, San Vincenzo, near the valley bot-tom. His belly too big, his smile ingratiating, seeming to say, "Bring me your money and your sins will be forgiven, but you will have to continue being inconvenienced with differ-ent mass times, while I struggle to fit three churches into my hectic schedule". This schedule is necessary because the

Diocese will not sink any more money into the older churches. It is not uncommon for a priest to circulate between four or five villages.

When assigning the funds, I wonder if the Diocese conveniently forgot the women, young, smooth and supple, old, gnarled and arthritic, who crawled on their hands and knees in penance up the cold steps? Did the Diocese forget how these women, while their men were working or away at war, physically carried rocks up the hill to rebuild the campanile, the east wall, and the now empty priest's house? Perhaps the Diocese did not remember how one family, Guilio's family, donated the land for the cemetery, such an integral part of the villagers' lives.

With these not so meditative thoughts shrouding me in unhappiness, I walked down the little trail to the road and followed the small group of people who were making their way from the furthest houses, toward the church. A continual flow, a growing procession wends its way up the hill, past the cemetery and down to the church piazza. Greetings are dull and passionless. Some handshaking, some kissing on cheeks, first right then left, no clashing noses. That is reserved for the new-world visitors, the uninitiated.

The cheeks of the children, subjected so often to Nonas' and Zias' pinching, have become pink and round like little apples. Dressed like little princes and princesses, the girls wear frills and lace and ribbons of pale virginal colors, ears shining with gold studs, little black patent shoes iced with frilly white socks. The boys wear perfect little suits, black and austere with bow ties round their collars done up tight to the chin. The youngest cling to their mamas and peer up at the doting grandmas. Others run back and forth, excited, playful, for now the only true joy to grace this group of dour looking villagers. The older children, boys, of course, are behind the scenes, preparing robes, altars, candles, the magic of mass.

The women wear scarves tied piously over heads, cardigans

perfectly buttoned over their only Sunday best blouse, skirts neatly smoothed to knee, not above, and not below. Legs hairy, piano legs, bowed legs, stick legs, shapely legs, muscled calves, feet stuck into black church shoes, ankles overflowing, standing the pain in these perfectly polished torture traps, just for the Virgin Mary. God Bless Her.

The men in their groups, talking men stuff, the women fussing like hens trying to get them into church, in place, and in time for the mass, just as they have been doing for hundreds of year. And the men, their heads topped with fedoras, ignoring the clucking hens just as they have done for hundreds of years. Frayed shirt collars buttoned to the neck, no tie, with best Sunday suit threadbare but pressed to perfection. Of course Francesco had to check the tractor first and Marietta will kill him when she sees his oily handprints stamped across his rump. And she will not wait until they are home. She will berate him in front of the whole village. If he is really lucky he will escape into mass before she spots the oily backside, some respite at least from that raucous voice.

Entering the church, ladies to the right, men to the left. Take your pews please, and prepare your knees for the assaults of up-down, up-down, up-down. As the priest downs his third goblet of Christ's blood this morning even his cheeks are looking like rosy apples. As Luigi was at the church for his yearly visit, I decided to join him. The bone hard pews and what I perceived to be total dullness were worth enduring if I could gaze around this sweet little church. I thought about our leather hassocks at Sunday school when I was a child, as my bony knees found no comfort on the wooden kneeling boards attached to the back of each pew. Pleasure was to be found in the beauty of the old church, the cracking frescoes, the marble figures at the tops of the pillars, huge oil paintings of the Madonna and Jesus, and of Saint Peter. Even in this semi-poverty there is real beauty, feelings of peace emanate from the walls, the ceiling, as the incense wafts across the congregation.

After the solemn service, the joyous exit is wonderful as the church disgorges its contents into the sunny piazza. Is this the same somber crowd that assembled here an hour ago? There is much smiling, many toothless grins, and laughter. Huge voices out-shouting each other as if in argument, but simply trying as always to be heard above the rest. The men continue to discuss the problems, but in a more lighthearted manner now, after all it is Sunday. One old codger says, "How can we make a living off the land? No one wants to buy our hay, our milk".

"Well, the local government is to blame for everything" says another, "some of us now have only one or two cows. What is the point of herding them all the way to the fields every day? We leave them tethered in their stalls."

Old Alberto says, "Well it is the new animal rights' laws. They say we cannot keep animals without light and fresh air, so we are just waiting for them to die."

"Yes", says Franco, "and did you hear that you are only allowed to keep a certain number of birds in a cage depending on its size, and so many fish per tank? What's this country coming to?"

"And those rich folk coming up from the city at weekends. They just bring trouble and noise with those kids roaring around on dirt bikes", complains another, "And I don't like that woman up there, either. Don't talk to her. I saw her talking to a polizia de finanza. I know she's looking for our receipts in the waste bins".

But through it all they manage to come out laughing and smiling, the weight of their sins lifted from their shoulders for another week.

Having dutifully made the appropriate farewells for today at least, I wandered back up to the cemetery to say hello to Nona and to freshen her flowers, leaving Luigi gossiping with the villagers. Cemeteries are places of great interest to me. Provided with little glimpses into the past, I always come away with a resolve to experience more, to see more, but

never to end up in a hole in the ground, or in a box in a wall.
I would want to be free and can imagine my ashes, my soul,
flying away over the Emilian hills. As usual, attempting to
improve my knowledge about family lines and connections,
I wandered around the cemetery of Rovinaglia, this crooked
old piece of ground, covered with leaning head stones, some
stacked against the walls, bones long since removed, people,
families forgotten. I see Ferraris and Doras, Castalottis, and
Di Vincenzos; I see tiny faded photographs stuck to headstones with eyes still peering out into the world. Dates that
reach back into history adorn headstones, telling of ancient,
tough old men who saw their second century, of boys who
went off to war and never came back, of women who toiled
away their lives, of children who succumbed to influenza,
and of babies who hardly took their first breaths. It is all
here. Years of living and dying wrapped in the old rock walls,
rocks hewn from the same earth to which these souls have
been consigned. Luigi's grandmother Carolina Castelotti, and
grandfather Luigi Dora, the man who built the family home
on the ruins of a previous house, now rest in this lovely peaceful place.

As I closed the old iron gates behind me and I walked down
between the banks of lavender, I could not help but admire
these people. A people who endured this difficult life, who
lost children so young, whose lives were torn asunder by wars,
by mans' inhumanity to man, and still the pattern continues.
My senses enveloped in the aroma of lavender, I thought
about Carolina and Luigi. The light was fading when I began my walk home and I ran the gauntlet of "bat alley". They
swooped down screeching just a few inches above my head.

The chef had been at work! We had dinner with a nice
glass of wine, and we talked about the lives of Carolina and
Luigi. Making the best life they were able for their children
and themselves, glossing over the misery, it might have been
a pleasurable way to live sometimes, but we could only imagine the backbreaking work involved in building the house.

Chiseling the rock, hewing the huge chestnut beams, grasping and straining with rough worn hands to place the rocks just so, the huge corner stones at perfect right angles, all built above the cantina, constructed centuries ago with awesome arches and nooks and crannies for storage of wine, root vegetables, cheese, milk, and for animal stalls. When Luigi and Carolina began to have children, the need arose for a bigger house. He built another rock house with stables and cantina beneath, kitty corner to their first house. This was the house in which my husband was born, but much, much later fell to rack and ruin and became "the dump". The dump is our piazza now.

The original cantina beneath Nona's house is now a place of darkness and of cobwebs and wood-wormy chestnut barrels, of huge cross beams, old farm tools, chains, iron pots, old furniture, demijohns with hand-hewn stoppers in hand woven baskets, and steamer trunks. I have stood and looked at these remnants of the past, and the steamer trunks particularly create an historic picture in my mind when the late 1800's and early 1900's the New World called.

Farmers' lives were packed in those trunks. Villagers left, in search of the good life, prosperity, jobs, and food. They went to London. They went to America. What a culture shock from fragrant meadows to concrete jungle. From red tiled roofs to red brick walkups with stinking hallways. They went from horse and cart and tractor, to trolleys, trams, cars, trucks and buses; from congenial gatherings in the piazza to the anonymity of one among the masses, to racial prejudice and rejection of immigrants. These tough and resilient, emotional people endured the trans-Atlantic passage in crowded, stinking ships, stuffed below deck, men and boys separated from the wives, moms and sisters. They were following the dream perpetuated by those who went before.

In the 1950's, times were hard on the northern Italian farmland. Luigi's parents made the decision to emigrate to New York where his father, Lorenzo, had a brother, and other

family members had gone some years before. The journey
began with the train to Genoa and then transferring to the
ship to take them on their adventure. For some reason they
were not allowed to board the ship and had to wait for the
next one. The cramped and uncomfortable crossing on the
"Conte Biancomano" did not seem so awful when on landing
in New York they heard the terrible news of the sinking of
the "Andrea Doria", the ship on which they were originally
booked.

As the great unwashed emerged from the bowels of the
boat papers were issued, luckier people were received by
anxious relatives, others went on their own lonely ways to
boarding homes, struggling with little or no command of this
new language. Life was very different for the immigrants.
Most were able to adapt to the new, frantic way of life but
some could not shake the bonds of the old country. Lorenzo
was a quiet, peaceful person. Perhaps the rush and mayhem
of New York was too overpowering for him. As family ten-
sion built to a crescendo he returned to Italy while Luigi and
his mother went to stay with Nona's other daughter in England who was established and married and living in a town
not far from where my family lived.

It was at this time in 1964, after several more wonderful
family camping holidays and dreams of Italy still on our
minds, my sister and I decided to visit the International Club
in a town nearby. Designed to host the Greeks, Italians, Span-
iards and foreigners working mostly in the service trades, it
was a meeting place where the workers could connect with
home. I spied a handsome, shy young man at the club, but
being shy myself, I was not about to go and talk to him. The
next day I made sure to be at the El Toucan coffee bar, where
some of these handsome fellows met and there he was in the
corner, protected it seemed by several others. This went on
for a few weeks until I heard via the grapevine that he wanted
to ask me out. Looking back, I cannot imagine from where I
drew the courage to approach him and ask if he would like

to go to a movie with me, but I did. The romance progressed. I remember being on the bus with my mother and passing Luigi strolling along, I turned to her and said, so she tells me, "There's the man I'm going to marry". Perhaps she remembers it so distinctly because she and my father were not at that time aware of our relationship. English people loved to take their daughters for holidays in Italy but they certainly did not want their daughters to marry foreigners. I endured the wrath of my father but slowly, I am sure after my mother's advice, he began to accept the idea of our relationship.

We were married in 1966 and planned to move into a new flat with Luigi's mother, Angelina. I discovered that my mother-in-law was a very strong person in character and I was not at liberty to make any decisions regarding our home. I became frustrated, she did, I nagged Luigi, he nagged his mother, she nagged me. It was a wild, miserable time for me. Luigi was more rattled than I knew—one day he burned his pay packet in the fire without realizing he had not extracted the money. Tough week that one! My parents had rented our house and gone off on a trip round Europe and North Africa. I had no one to confide in but my poor husband. Then, a stroke of luck!

At that time in England, Canada was advertising heavily for immigrants. "We need you, we want you, if you can work hard you will make a great living in a wonderful country. You can own your own home, you can have a car and a summer cottage in the country." All this sounded so wonderfully tempting. The gold at the end of the rainbow! We were both keen on discovering more, so off we went to Canada House in London. Six months later we were boarding a flight from Heathrow to Montreal and to our new life. Time has been good to us, having finally settled in British Columbia (we left Quebec after five years because of the political unrest, which prompted the FLQ crisis, a movement working toward the separation of Quebec from Canada). Finally, after two children, working like demons, even achieving ownership of a summer cottage, moving hither and thither round the Province because of Luigi's work, and becoming total workaholics we seemed to fall apart with stress. Luigi had a mental breakdown and I was diagnosed with metastatic breast cancer, these crises occurring within the same month, January, 1995. It took time but eventually we sat back with huge sighs and contemplated life as sick retirees. The void of having nowhere to rush off to at eight o'clock each morning did not take long to overcome. The lack of constant beeping of Luigi's pager even when he was in the bathroom was never missed. We were actually surviving. The situation improved, we contemplated travel, the gym, cross-country skiing—there was so much to enjoy.

We had often talked about going back to Europe and now was our opportunity to take a leisurely trip as opposed to rushing stressfully through a two or three-week vacation break from the office. Knowing one does not have to return to the frantic workday makes a holiday far more enjoyable.

Angelina, the strong old Italian matriarch whom we thought would live forever because of her ability to fight back from yearly influenza and pneumonia, had died a number of years prior to our retirement. A rift had occurred between her two daughters, Meri and Lena, of which we were unaware. Squabbling had been going on for some time between them regarding Angelina's property, her land, her house. Luigi was slowly drawn into the melee as first one sister would call him and then the other, with their complaints about each other. We both realized that he did not appear anyway in the equation. We wondered why? During her lifetime, Nona had made verbal requests and bequeathments regarding her property and possessions, but had not drawn up a will, nothing was on paper. As the sisters continued their battle, Luigi realized he did have "a say" in matters upon discovering that Nona wanted him to have her house, No. 17, Rovinaglia. It was quite apparent that obtaining legal advice would be the only way to achieve resolution.

And so began the saga of establishing legal ownership of the land, the house, barns, crumbling sheds and falling-down cottages. Passed down through the generations by word of mouth, huge areas of meadows and woodlands had been carved down into smaller parcels and these were in contention also.

It strikes me now that we were pathetically innocent as we jumped into the churning depths of Luigi's family. We had no idea of how much effort we would have to make just to reason with his sister, let alone arrive at an amicable solution. Much diplomacy and patience was demanded of Luigi when he was boiling inside about nonsensical details that threatened to pull all asunder. Frustration was my enemy. With so little knowledge of the language I was often left hanging, puzzled, confused.

This day was to be one of negotiations. I really did not want anything to do with the meetings but I felt Luigi needed some moral support so I would go with him. Today it went on and on, like a ricocheting ball, from one person to another, back and forth. I might have been at a tennis match as my eyes went from side to side to side. Enough, I thought, they are all mad. I left quickly and returned to the house.

I scrubbed and cleaned and swept, and lit the fire in the old Aga to fend off the winds as they flew over the hills from Tuscany with a vengeance. It appeared those Tuscan war lords were angry, the sky blackened, it roiled and boiled its billowing mass of clouds, the distant rumbles and a far off flash heralded what was to come. The wind screamed through the rafters, throwing tiles around as if they were leaves, woofing under the door and through the cracks. My God, this was worse than winter in Canada, and it was already June. Global warming and changing weather patterns aside, this was ridiculous!

The house had, however, endured for centuries. Everything the elements could throw at it made no difference. With meter thick walls it was not going anywhere. Neither was I. Sitting outside with my coffee as long as I dared, I jumped out of my skin as a huge bang rocked the world directly overhead. Lightning carved up the sky like pieces of pie. The power failed. As the noise and light show abated God emptied his buckets. Down came the rain in driving sheets whipping this way and that in the ferocious wind. Lashing at the house and beating at the shutters, it squeezed its way through the slats and between the poor old window frames. It ran down the old plastered walls, feeling quite at home as it simply followed the same path worn through the different layers of plaster and paint from years of previous storms. Water collected in puddles on the warped old chestnut floor, dripping between the boards into the cantina below.

I had forgotten to bring in my beautiful geraniums and begonias from the balcony. Looking out of the kitchen door I could see their poor pathetic blossoms smashed to pulp. The line of washing hung in soggy, dripping fashion, begging to be rescued. It would have to stay outside. There was nowhere to hang it but on the back of wood-wormy chairs or on the poky steel rods sticking out around the chimney waiting to jab Canadian giants in the eye.

Peace returned and the marine mist slithered over the hilltops like something from a Dracula movie, billowing, wafting, and swallowing the churches and villages whole, digesting, then spitting them out into spaces in the mist. It would continue now for two days. A pattern set perhaps at the beginning of time. A warming wind to follow, as the Mediterranean takes pity on the poor cold mountain villages, pushing its warm clear air over the hills.

Everything will appear more colorful, fresher and crisper. The flowers will stand up to attention, the battered leaves will wave happily. The lizards will appear from between the rocks and bask, some tailless, their last basking not beyond the reach of the stray cats. Cats, lean and with voracious appetites, attacking with lightning speed often only to be rewarded with a wriggling tail that fools them just long enough, allowing the lizard to escape and grow a new defense mechanism. Out will come our sun chairs, the umbrella and picnic table. The hammock will soothe its occupant in a gentle sway between the walnut and apple tree. Paperbacks and newspapers will alternately be read and then lie on the grass as the Canadians snooze and the curious villagers will be reinforced in their thoughts of how odd we are.

Ignoring the storm, the meeting in the garage had continued. However, now duly adjourned by Madam Chairwoman, Luigi had returned. His head cracking, frustrated, he'd had enough. "They have minds as narrow as yellow lines. You can't reason with Meri. She's like a brick wall. She will not give an inch. It is her way or no way". On and on he goes, venting his frustration. Did we really believe we would have the paperwork signed, sealed and settled this year? We want to do things to renovate the house but dare not. What if we never have it? What if the powerful women in this family trample their polite brother? Wear him down until he no longer cares, until he wants no more to do with any of them. Nothing that we do is missed. The eyes are not evident, but they are there. Am I becoming totally paranoid?

We spend hours and days cleaning up outside. The lower level of the old ruined house next door, the house where Luigi and his siblings were born, is still partially standing. As with most of the old houses built into the hillsides, the rear wall is the steeply sloping bedrock. The front wall, facing out across the valley, is still intact. Built into the hillside it is level with the land now, but the east wall drops about twenty feet to its base below. The two side-walls have partially collapsed in on themselves but the piles of rock are retrievable and eventually Luigi would rebuild the walls under the very critical eyes of his nephew who is an expert on rock walls. As always, Luigi does everything his own way. I am sure all the men had a chuckle in the garage when they talked about his stone mason skills. But for now there it all sat, a forlorn shell. A dump filled with old bed springs, old stoves and pipes, cracked china sinks, plastic buckets, bits of broken furniture, dented kettles, bottles, baskets, and old farm tools. We waded around in it, our hearts sorry for what once was. The nettles and brambles fought to retain their hold on the few bits and pieces we tried to salvage. How sad it all seemed now. Part of a long forgotten time.

We sat on the wall for some time, contemplating the mess. Looking out across the valley, the wonderful view was soothing. Luigi slipped into his inevitable stories of the old family. A family tree so convoluted and intertwined like a tropical rain forest. I hack my way through the jungle of twisted vines and branches gasping for air, trying to reach the top. Determined to grasp and remember the names, I vow to bring pruning shears on my next encounter with Luigi's inexorable account of his family. Somewhere, in the year dot, these people began. Just when I am sure I have grasped a line, more relatives leap from the branches. And grandpa Luigi and grandmother Carolina begat Angelina, Guiseppe, Marietta and Agostino, who begat Jackie and Linda and Eugenia and Meri and Lena and Luigi, who begat Veronica and Remo and Aurora and Gianni and Roberto and Stefano and Giorgio and Guiliana and Carlo and Melody, some of whom are still begetting. But wait, Angelina married Lorenzo and they are related. How can that be? Somewhere in the annals of time, their ancestors crossed paths and so on and on we go. I will be taken to meet this uncle, that cousin, twice removed, introduced to Zias and Cougini. I will meet long lost cousins seventeen times removed who have arrived from the States.

Our peace is broken as a Scottish brogue hails us from the fields, another twig on the tree. Ah, that's the "Scott's Porridge Oats lady"—name association? Forget it, I just remember the association. There is "Cow Bruno" and "Brown Bruno" not to be confused with Cousin Bruno; the "Paintbrush Man", the "Sad Lady", the "Tractor Boy". There are also the "Dog Man", the "Cat Lady", "Popeye" and "Early Gray".

I have long since leapt from the family tree. I think of my own roots, William the Conqueror intertwined in them somewhere, but they seem a mere sapling in comparison to this monstrous jungle of lives. After all this family history, quite enough to boggle my mind, we finish our work for the day. With backs broken, sweaty, grime streaked faces, we manage a giggle among the groans of pain. Tomorrow we will continue to clean up, to find stuff to fill the gaping remains of that poor old house. Our plan was to repair the walls, fill the whole lot level with the tops of those walls and make a little piazza where we could sit in the sun, sip wine, drink cappuccino and do those things that are an integral part of this life.

Dinner brings more stories of family and villagers. Tales once, twice, thrice told, handed down over time, grow and blossom into larger more exciting, more intricate stories. This would be a typical dinnertime, a lovely meal cooked by Luigi, our favorite wines and total relaxation. This dinnertime I was treated to a story about the strange old man called Ricobon who had lived in the clump of houses call Brattesani, down the hillside just below us. During and after the war he continually demanded police protection because he was a fascist and was convinced the partisans were after him. The caribinieri were constant visitors and the villagers wished they would just take him away. His paranoia never assured him of his safety. He died a miserable old man, alone in his old cottage. No wonder he was a bit odd, poor old thing, they say he had a hole in his head and would show the children of the village his throbbing brain.

I was also treated this evening to the story about the old man who practiced witchcraft. After the war he went to California for a number of years and the villagers say he lived with a group of native Indians and this is where he picked up his wickedness. After returning to Rovinaglia he began his black magic rituals. He set up an altar in his house and would place his pet chicken upon it proceeding to have lengthy discussion with the hen. He would also sit up in the cemetery making piles of a mixture of sand, clay, and salt and chant and perform rituals as he read the bible. He was blamed for every disaster that befell the community. The villagers said that the storms would come, there was too much rain, not enough rain, too much wind, too hot, too cold, too damp, too cloudy, loss of hay, small eggs, early winters, late springs, almost everything that went wrong was attributed to him and his wretched chicken.

I can personally relate to how stories can grow and flourish over the years. My own husband in the telling, often, of his childhood to his children, went from, "The nearest town, Borgotaro is quite a long way away", to "It was an overnight trip just to get there let alone return, my mother would pack food baskets for me, I took a blanket to sleep under the chestnut trees at night." Years later the kids and I had such a giggle as we discovered it was only six kilometers, an hour or so walk. We still tease him about that. He has never since to this day, walked down to Borgotaro.

※ ※ ※

It is Monday, market day. Great preparation takes place for this weekly event. It is the highlight of the week for the ladies of the village. They primp and preen, hair is washed, curlers lovingly placed and wrapped safely in cotton scarves, the lumpy sleepless night endured. The best frock resurrected once more, the church cardigan buttoned once again. Gather the shopping bags, the faithful umbrella, for if it should rain, you would not want to get wet because then you would catch a cold or maybe influenza or even pneumonia. Meri and Giulio always go alone. She will not share a car with the other women, so much a loner and independent. The other old folks squeeze into the little cars and descend the six kilometers into the town, into the 20th century. A joyous gathering of Monday morning happiness, which seems to gradually lessen during the week until Sunday arrives and the ritual churchgoing once more invigorates them.

The travelling stalls arrive early. At six o'clock in the morning they roll into their weekly-allotted spots between the great London Plane trees on Viale Bottega, street of the market, that have sheltered generations of markets. What stories these trees could tell of bartering, dealing, and complaints, of gossiping groups and busy mamas stocking up for the week. Of squalling lambs and upside down flapping chickens, calves and cows and gobbling turkeys, and soft sweet bunnies all on their journeys to hell. These days the Planes are happier. The times of the livestock markets are gone with the introduction of the new animal rights legislation more sensitive to the welfare of our co-dwellers on this planet. The trees sway their gorgeous leaves above the white vans, tin box things void of personality, dead nothings. But wait, they live, the sides are thrown open, the colored awnings unfurled, the merchants and their wares burst from within. Tables, stalls, racks are erected. Shoes, buckets, carpets, can openers, plastic crosses, glass ashtrays and much more to satisfy the needs of any self-respecting mama. Hanging clothes brush the heads of the early throng. No orderly queuing. Shouting and pushing for the best bargains, get in, get out and on to the cheese stall, the vegetables and fruit. Shout louder, a cacophony of sound, liberally seasoned with music blaring from an old man's stand, and tapes of accordion music, scratchy tenors of yesteryear, long since consigned to the garbage by the younger generation. All this is wrapped in an aroma of sweat, cigarette smoke, and cologne, the smelly Parmesan adding just the right mix to gag the uninitiated. The process complete for another week, the women scuttle away, their elbow joints stretched beyond repair, arms bearing bags sprouting cabbages, garlic, tea towels, plastic flowers, and toilet brushes.

The men have collected at their favorite bar on the corner at the end of the Viale Bottega, awaiting the arrival of the women. An impenetrable crowd of card players, smoking, drinking espresso, tossing back a quick aperitif. Others, standing in groups, passing the time of day. The same old stories, the same old Monday morning conversations. Cigarettes dangling from lips, from yellow stained fingers, eyes screwed up, faces wrinkled, stray smoke assaulting nostrils. Sixty, seventy, a hundred men, solving the world's problems, invincible, in to- tal control, until their women arrive. These puffed up rooster-men, these warriors, deflate when claimed by their women. Shrinking, submissive, doddering old men, laden with plastic bags, are herded away by the tough little ladies, stuffed into tiny cars, retreating to the hills until next Monday.

Meanwhile back in the market, the next shift browses. Townsfolk, the mothers and babies, toddlers underfoot, run- ning here and there with no fear of predators, just doting Italians loving their children, the heart of all Latin families. Workers on their morning break, visiting soccer players, aim- less wanderers with nothing else to do this morning, and the younger set.

Have genetics created these beautiful young people? The young women, lithe sashaying bodies, perfectly formed fig- ures encased in silky lycra, so tight were they poured into those pants? —no cellulite, no lumps and bumps and rolls, perhaps a little silicone here and there. Tanned arms, beauti- fully manicured hands reaching to stroke the swaying curtains of gorgeous sweaters, long slinky skirts, lacy sexy undies. No bargaining, no screaming back and forth, simply hand- ing over thousands of lire without a second thought. The young men saunter in groups, arms draped around shoul- ders, open signs of affection for their friends, hips swaying in Armani jeans. Are drop dead gorgeous looks a prerequi- site for the Italian male? Eyes deep, mysterious, flashing and naughty, scanning every inch of female anatomy. No politi- cal correctness here, just open appreciation of the gorgeous females. No twittering and giggling from the girls as their equally appreciative glances are returned.

I walk up one side of the market and down the other, being

sure not to miss a stall. I need a few small things for the house, some hooks, a ball of twine, tea towels and a dustpan and brush. In fact I need too many things but I must adjust to this way of life. I can do without, I can "make do and mend"! Two hours later I am still enthralled, as I will continue to be for many Mondays. I leave with huge yellow silk sunflowers, a definite necessity that will look gorgeous in an old green glass demijohn rescued from beside a garbage can. I am weighed down with much more than I intended. Ropes of huge garlic corms, the heaviest kilo ever carved of real, solid Parmigiano. A wonderful plump, purple melanzzane (egg-plant), more geraniums, even a bunch of flowers for that fearful little woman whom I actually secretly admire for her steadfast ability to endure, to cater to every need of her family, to fend off interlopers come what may.

I leave the market and pass through a now smaller crowd of men who are still gathered in the piazza in front of the bar and seem to fall aside in shock as I stride straight through the middle of them all. Sorry guys, I want the shortest route to my favorite outdoor café, Maria's Pizzaria, where I will wait for Luigi. Eventually they will accept the tall Canadian but for now they seem shocked at my apparent brazenness. I walk through cobbled streets and alleyways to via Nazionale. I never cease to be in awe of these cool, shady streets, carved between the tall buildings. Ochre, yellow, sienna walls reaching skyward, joined together to form solid façades along the streets. Clinging to the walls are colored shutters and balconies dripping with geraniums. Lines of washing linking opposite sides of the narrow streets, decorated with an array of old ladies' bloomers and bras, lacy little things daughters bought at the market, holey old undershirts, socks, tablecloths and dish rags, all on display for the world to see.

These handsome old buildings were once the 16th and 17th century palazzos of the great families of the region, Boveri, Bertucci, Corsini-Manara. Visiting royalty often graced these palazzos with their presence, Landi and Fieschi, Dukes of

Lavagna, Marie Luigia of Austria, Elizabetta Farnese on route to her marriage to King Philip V of Bourbon. Behind the walls lie the inner courtyards, gardens, and elaborate stone patterned paths. Arched porticos supported by marble pillars surround the courtyards with stone and marble stairways leading up to first, second, and third floor walkways. Tall doors open into high, cool salons, frescoes decorating their domed ceilings, electric cables stretched hither and thither across angels and voluptuous women draped seductively as they look down upon the 20th century.

Archaeological findings in and around Borgotaro indicate that the town's history reaches as far back as the 5th Millennium B.C. Etruscan ruins can be found in this area as they can across northern Italy. Broadening its empire, Rome began to overcome the Etruscan centers about two hundred years before Christ. Borgotaro represented a strategic position at the junction of three regions, Emilia Romagna, Etrusca, from which originated the name Tuscany, and Liguria. The Romans had forged passes across the mountains, giving access to these regions. Borgotaro's economy improved as merchants, armies, travelers, and wandering tribes crossed these passes and took their cultures and influences to others. Access to Central Italy, the East Coast, and France improved trade and communication.

Historical records show that sometime during 900 A.D. a church was built at the confluence of the rivers Taro and Tarodine. The community of Toresano grew around this site. Some inhabitants began to settle further westward and a separate community grew across the river. It became known as Borgo Val di Taro, "Town in the Valley of the Taro". The original fortress had its origins in an 11th century community run by the monks of Bobbio who led a very simple, uncomplicated way of life. This was not to last as throughout the centuries to follow the town was conquered and owned by different warring dukes, Landi and Fieschi families such as, Visconti, Sforza, Doria and Farnese. Even the popes and the

Council of Piacenza would get their greedy little paws into the fray. In the 12th century, Henry VI dropped by en route to Naples from Milan. So impressed was he with the unique setting of the Fortress in the Valley that he declared its name to be official. It would not change until its 20th century inhabitants began to call it Borgotaro. The old town that we see now was built around the church of San Antonino, the first stone for which was laid in 1650. Inside San Antonino is a wealth of beauty and history. An amazing wooden pulpit with carved wooden statues and ornate inset panels, a high altar of white marble towers over those who kneel before it, a magnificent organ issues tones from one thousand and eight hundred organ pipes.

Because of the town's strategic position, ownership continued to ricochet between Dukes and Princes. Early in the 14th century, the then current Duke of Landi, Agostino, took control. He ordered the destruction of the beautiful city wall encircling the town. Apparently he was quite convinced that rival factions within, were planning an uprising and without the walls the naughty rebels would be in full view standing around in the piazzas discussing his overthrow. But of course like all good rebels they went underground, secreted away down dark cobbled alleyways, in cantinas and behind shuttered windows. In any event he need not have bothered because the Visconti armies performed a successful invasion and tossed him out.

Between 1322 and 1335, the papal domination involved Borgotaro's submission into the Holy See and then once again the battling began between the dukes, and the town changed hands four or five times. Finally in 1578, fed up with so many regimes, the people took control of their own town and sent the princes and dukes on their way. Through free choice, the people chose Octavio Farnese to be their prince, and for almost two hundred years there was little oppression and the townsfolk felt quite secure and settled. With no male heir, the dynasty ended in 1731. The dukedom was passed into the hands of Carlo Borbone, son of Elizabetta Farnese, and so began years of Borbone rule.

During his Italian Campaign in 1796-97, Napoleon Buonaparte came marching through at the head of his troops, his high black boots creating the image of a man larger than life, or a fashion faux pas. He was successful in annexing parts of Italy, thereby breaking the then current Austrian stranglehold. Consequently this poor little town was once again kicked around like a football, changed hands, and became part of the French Empire.

Oppressed people do not sit around for too long before rebelling and the early 1800's brought revolution. Italy's greatest hero in the making, Garibaldi, led the forces towards a united Italy and in 1860 the kingdom of Italy was born. Kings were crowned and sat on the throne, comfy in the thought of a secure future for the monarchy. Well of course all good things come to an end—the royal bottoms warmed the royal throne until 1946 when the Christian Democrats voted in favor of an Italian Republic. King Victor Emanuel III abdicated and his son, Humbert II, ascended the throne, but was made short shrift of and was sent off to exile.

Through all the centuries of madness and mayhem of battles and world wars, of partisans and Nazis and Fascists, Borgotaro has plodded on her steady way through history, wall-less and perhaps not as beautiful as some historical centers, she retains an old-world charm, unspoiled by hype and commercialism. A charm enhanced and perpetuated by her people. The weekends and evenings bring out the crowds. Families stroll back and forth along the cobbled via Nazionale. Dads, moms, grandparents, teenagers, children running back and forth, playing free from the danger of traffic which is banned from the town center for the summer. The cafes and bars are full of coffee and aperitif drinkers, and of course many walkers lick at the inevitable gelati, the best ice cream in the world.

Beneath an archway on my way to the via Nazionale, I

encounter one of my favorite people from our village. Paolino, dressed to kill, his red bandana tied saucily round his neck, sparkling white shirt open just enough to reveal a thick gold chain and crucifix nestling on a hairy chest. Hands casually resting in pockets of beautiful brown pants, which flow down to soft, Italian leather shoes. His handsome brown face breaks into a huge mustachioed smile, showing perfect white teeth. Out come his hands to relieve me of my bags. The traditional cheek to cheek greeting is performed. He rattles on in that incomprehensible dialect and I smile and nod accordingly, not understanding one word. He insists on helping me to the cafe where we dump the bags on the chairs under the trees. The other Paolino whom I know, is a toothless, weathered man who wears a dirty old hat and a ragged, frayed t-shirt, shorts with holes in the seat and big farm boots, laced to the calf and topped by home made wooly socks. The faithful red bandana round his neck and the twinkling saucy eyes are the only clues I have to help me in recognition. The smile, of course is ever present, the Sunday-Monday teeth absent. He drives his tractor back and forth between house and field, hauling hay and firewood. His routine never changes and his siesta is spent resting against his barn with a bottle of red wine, enjoying his beloved piece of Emilia Romagna. He is very proud of his children who attend university. He is even more proud of his lovely wife who is seldom seen, but feeds stray cats, milks one lonely cow, and makes cheese and bread. Every evening they regularly enjoy a little decadence and down tiny chocolatey pastries dripping with cream for which Paolino drives downtown each morning. Of course that also allows him time to coffee with his buddies, another entrenched part of his daily routine.

Secure in the knowledge that my bags will remain safely on the chairs I leave them and the nodding sunflowers and go into the bar to buy my "droga", my daily drug of choice, my cappuccino. Having been warned by my ever travelling expert-on-Italy daughter that I will pay more for coffee if it is served at the table, I remain standing at the bar ready to hand over my 2000 lire. The lady, whom I discover later to be Maria's daughter, insists I return to my table and she follows me out carrying the cappuccino. She says that I should pay when I leave. It will still only be 2000 lire. Oh, the joys of small town Italy.

Maria's Café is situated on a piazza at the Portello. The Portello is an arched entranceway into the old town, at the top of the steps leading up from the main road. This road circles most of the town and in part runs along the top of what once was the old city wall. The chairs and tables are set out on the cobbled piazza beneath huge Plane trees. The Piazza is partially surrounded by some of the 15th century Palazzos which front onto via Nazionale, the main street. The old entrance to the town through the archway of the Portello is set at the rear of the piazza and is best known as a rendezvous point. The whole of Borgotaro seems to meet here at one time or another. School kids to be picked up for their ride home, young men and women meeting before going off to the gym or on to a bar. The Monday crowd waiting for rides home after the market, bank managers, surveyors, teenagers, and farmers. All manner of bottoms have graced the stone steps while waiting.

On one occasion several of us were standing around in Meri's farmyard discussing how I might walk down to the town via shortcuts through the fields. I could spend the day drawing and then meet with Giuliana to drive me back up to Rovinaglia. In my ignorance of the beautiful Italian language I suggested to Giuliana that she meet me at four o'clock at the Bordello. Roars of laughter erupted as she explained my faux pas to the listeners.

The Portello is an inspirational setting in which to draw or paint and I have often added to my memories with drawings

Virginia Gabriella Ferrari

done at Maria's tables. I was asked by her son-in-law, the pizza maker, to do a painting of the building housing the café. Maria's old man would come out and check my progress and throw his arms up in the air "Piu colore signora", he would shout, "more color, more color". It was alien to me, being a rather wishy-washy watercolorist. Attempting to fulfil his wishes, my picture became a work of horror to me. I could hardly add my signature to the painting and was pleased not to see it hanging in the restaurant. I later discovered, however, that when the family gave it to Maria, matted and framed, she refused to hang it anywhere but in pride of place over her sideboard in their house. Today, though, was the pleasant experience of quick sketches, capturing stances, gestures, expressions of the Borgotarese, drinking cappuccino and watching the world go by.

Luigi arrived from a meeting with the surveyor, Mussi. This man was in my opinion, quite remarkable. He handled all the legal stuff and visits back and forth between the land commission office, the town hall, the Forestry department, Rovinaglia, Parma. I only ever saw him once with a tape measure, stumbling around in a steeply sloping field below the house. Perhaps surveyors the world over do much more than my stereotypical image would have them do. I thought they stood at the side of Canadian highways with tripod scope things or measured city lots.

Shaking his head and emitting a huge sigh, Luigi sat at the table and I thought what now? We were aware of other members of Nona's family still living. However, assuming that her spoken word would be enough to assure Luigi of eventual legal ownership of the house, he was surprised to hear it would be his responsibility to provide the names and addresses of eight people, his cousins, who were spread from one end of the globe to the other. I suppose it simply boiled down to, if you want the house you can do the legwork. Luigi had had no contact with most of them since he left Italy at age fifteen, heading for New York on that stinking ship. If his responsibility of searching for the cousins was not enough, after providing this information to the surveyor and the surveyor officially apprising the cousins of the situation, there would be a twelve month period during which time the cousins could contest Nona's wishes. We did not even want to contemplate what might ensue should one, or any number of them, make claim on the house. I could imagine the house being carved up, a bit for this cousin, a bit for that cousin, and a bit for another, and nothing left but the doormat.

The ownership of Nona's land had never been in question. Luigi and his other sister understood that Meri and her family had worked every hay field, cutting, raking, turning, baling, stacking. They had ploughed acres of land, planted potatoes and corn, bending, digging, hand sorting, boxing, storing. Years of crushing and grinding corn, of cutting, sawing, chopping and stacking firewood. From the day they married fifty-five years ago, Meri and her husband, and later her boys, and her daughter, had broken their backs on this land. Luigi's only desire, which seemed pitiful considering the amount of land and how much lay fallow becoming overgrown brambly jungles, was to have three small pieces. What, in fact, was perhaps ten or twelve acres among a thousand or more had fallen prey to his sentimental memories of childhood. Of helping his father tend the terraced vineyards, of driving the livestock up to the summer pastures and staying up there in the thatched cottage, the family in one small room. Of climbing trees, and hunting snakes, and looking for old grenades and ammunition hidden in the hills. Of unexploded shells embedded in the earth, one of which blew his friend's hand off during one of these escapades, but his memory dimmed the horror and produced one of those great childhood adventures. Even so, it would be difficult for Meri to concede even these small pieces to her brother.

Luigi spent most of the last few days of our holiday, talking with the old people in Rovinaglia and in his father's village of San Vincenzo. Any information might help his efforts to establish contact with those long lost cousins.

CHAPTER III

1997

Once we were back at home in Canada, we began the awesome task of tracking down the cousins in America, Australia,
Scotland, and England. We almost gave up at one point when
we were not as successful as we had hoped. But a bright
spark appeared from the Scottish countryside, Mario, a son
of Guiseppe, one of Nona's brothers. He was lovely—he spent
a lot of time talking with Luigi on the phone and their relationship grew to the point where they promised to meet if we
should return to Europe.

I could never stay away from my Emilia and now I was
provided with the perfect ammunition to fuel my desire, egg-
ing Luigi on to visit Mario and his family. So tempting was it
now, eagerly wanting to renew old ties, to meet new lines of
the family! Plans began to gel for a spring visit to Italy.

We flew via London which gave us the opportunity to stay
with my brother and his family and also to go to Scotland.
After a ten-hour nightmare bus journey, which made the dear
old Greyhound seem like the Concorde, we arrived in
Glasgow, the grayest, dullest city I had ever set eyes upon.
Built mainly of granite, the city reflects little light, the feeling
of gloom is continual. We escaped from amid the gray buildings as Mario whisked us away in to the fresh light of the
countryside.

Walking round the village of Beith, it was easy to appreciate why so many Italians from northern Italy had migrated
to this part of the world. Years ago, sailors would jump ship
as the vessels took on their cargo of coal at Newcastle. Moving up the coastal areas and inland looking for work, the men

must have felt very much at home in the narrow cobbled streets and grey rock cottages of the villages, the hillsides rolling away into slate colored skies, the winds whipping across the heather. Then the sunny days, bringing out the old ladies with their brooms, the flower pots appearing, the smiles and cheery greetings. Wives and children followed from Italy and single men "cross pollinated" and whole communities began to establish themselves.

Gathering sufficient information from Mario and two other cousins in Scotland, we were able to establish that five were dead and three still existed. Five down and three to go was my thought! I could not shed tears for those I had never known.

After rushing round the British Isles like whirling dervishes all we wanted was to rest and restore. Arrival in Rovinaglia was delightful, once again I was overwhelmed with the beauty, the bewitching soul of Emilia—would I ever be released from her grasp? We passed the list of details regarding the living cousins on to the surveyor. In talking to two of those whom we had met, it appeared possible that one or both might want a share, that they might contest Nona's wishes regarding the house. The excitement built, as we believed the cousins would be contacted in short order and would make quick decisions. Our sails collapsed, windless, when it became obvious this was not high on Mussi's list of priorities. We wanted to enjoy our holiday and came to realize we had to put the whole issue away and get on with the more important things in life, enjoying the almost complete piazza, doing secret jobs in the house, quietly so neighbors would not report the banging to Meri. Oh the paranoia—we must cast it aside—we are not depressed Rovinaglians! And so we did.

My friend's daughter had traveled with us this year and did much to keep our minds in the moment. Sara, a typical teenager, was loaded with the usual teenage equipment, boom box, tapes, bike, clothes, clothes, and more clothes, enough

shoes to outfit an army and tons of correspondence courses
that she had to complete because of missing school. Try being a beautiful Canadian girl in Italy, a country full of
gorgeous guys. Not easy to be a dedicated student! She and
Gloria, Stefano and Anna's daughter, became friends. Often
the language barrier sent them into paroxysms of laughter
but it did not stop them from doing silly kid stuff together.
Spending hours away in the woods, coming back with cheeky
red clown mouths from spending too much time in the wild
cherry trees. Playing leapfrog on the top of the precipitous
wall. Cycling as fast as they could down to the other villages,
legs high in the air, screaming like banshees.

The summer approached. It was a lovely time to be in
Rovinaglia. Constant sun and warmth, a slow relaxed atmosphere settling in to the valley. There are always farmers in
their fields, jobs to do in the farmyard, but those things are
taken with a more laid back attitude as opposed to the fre-
netic pace of the late summer and autumn and preparation
for winter.

There is time for Meri and Giulio to mount their faithful
1950's Land Rover and rattle up the bumpy, uncomfortable
road to the cottage on Monte Pero. A traditional family gathering spot where her sons and their families will often meet
on the weekends, the place to which Luigi as a kid drove the
livestock for summer feeding. The various four-wheeled drive
vehicles arrived. Out poured the kids, dogs, eggplants, mushrooms, cheese, veal, milk and Coke, the Dads and Moms,
and two racked, broken, battered and bruised Canadians
having ridden up with Roberto and his family. I would prefer to make the next trip on my feet, it would be far more
comfortable.

Everything necessary to make an Italian family picnic was
being prepared. Old iron pots sizzled on top of the wood
stove, and Meri, up to her armpits in a huge pot of cornmeal
for the polenta, stirred with a big wooden stick. Mushrooms
and eggplant sizzled away, little fried potatoes with fresh

rosemary, crisp and brown and salty, the best in the world. Daughters-in-law bustled, preparing plates of proscuitto and parmesan, chunks of bread and torta di erbe. The men were outside setting up the trestles and planks of wood for the table and logs with planks on them for benches. From a secret source deep beneath the cottage, the wine appeared, and the bottles formed a row the length of the table, no fancy labels or gold sealed tops, just plain old grungy bottles filled with good red wine. An outdoor barbecue pit glowed with fiery-red embers. Above them on a rack, slabs of meat and for Zia Ginnie, the vegetarian, huge peppers and chunks of eggplant, and of course, porcini. Jam pies and pastries were set aside for later.

All the younger cousins were playing soccer, Giuliana, Andrea and Gloria, Anna and Stefano's brood, and Lorena and Francesca, Roberto and Rosetta's two girls, and of course, Sara. Luigi now joined the game and then Roberto and Stefano. It is funny how a family picnic can bring out the best in some people. Roberto, Meri's eldest son, is usually very serious and worried looking. He is very quiet and has a streak of family stubbornness. This day, however, he was leaping around with the kids and the football, laughing and playing like a schoolboy. Stefano, Meri's second oldest, was split between playing soccer and the barbecue and his same quiet smiling character remained with him. Georgio, Meri's youngest son, always has somewhere else to be. He's a wiry, small, strong-as-a-horse fellow, but has no time for anything but his construction business. To ever see him was a treat, to see him laughing and participating even for such a short time was so nice. Anna and Rosetta, the two wives, of course had priorities in the old kitchen and were unseen until the platters of food began to appear on the makeshift table.

No longer the enamoured center of attraction among her adoring younger female cousins because the men were now throwing themselves in to the fray, Giuliana left the maelstrom of tackling men and one tough Canadian girl, and joined me to sit on the little bench outside at the end of the cottage. At first just in silence, and then with halting stabs at each other's language we endeavored to get to know each other a little better. Discovering that she was P.M.Essing like crazy, I could now understand her moodiness. Certainly not a condition admitted to, or perhaps even recognized by the older generation here, she would suffer in silence, her moods misunderstood. Stuck up in the hills, isolated for most of the time from her friends downtown, trapped in a dismal cycle of repetitive misery and boredom, her temporary job at the office of the Justice of the Peace was her only lifeline to the outside world. Of course, what was so terribly unbearable today would seem inconsequential next week, when the blues had gone. Until next month, and the inevitable cycle would repeat itself. It was difficult not to continuously compare her life here to that of Sara's in Canada, who although some years younger, sometimes appeared more mature. Having a much larger slice of the world open to her she has matured more quickly, for good or bad. For the moment I tried to show support and understanding of Giuliana. My lecture about how beautiful she is and how there is a whole wide world waiting to be discovered would come another day when she was bouncing with energetic happiness—if I could just catch that moment. I suggested as often we had in the past, that she come to visit us in Canada perhaps with a friend, and for the first time I saw a spark of interest. I latched onto that and told her more about our beautiful Province. To many Italians living in rural Italy, Canada is Toronto and Montreal, RCMP, and Eskimos in igloos, and dreadful freezing weather. And of course we cannot make wine for a toffee! I cast a few hooks. How beautiful our beaches are between sparkling blue lakes, the vineyards lining the valley and the fruit orchards of cherries, apricots, peaches, apples and pears. And yes, we even have nightclubs where she can kick up her heels with her Canadian cousins. I reeled her in with an offer to pay for her flight. I did not allow myself to consider how we would find the money. There was something more important at stake. I could not bear to contemplate such youthful potential, wasting away to a life of drudgery like her mother. We both became excited discussing possible dates. I could not help thinking that she would change her mind, but continued to hope. As it turned out I would not be disappointed. In November of that year she and her delightful girlfriend did visit. Not the best time of the year in the Okanagan but at least an opportunity for them to experience our way of life, to see the world from a different viewpoint.

"Mangia, mangia" — "time to eat", shouted a hungry boy, and everyone gathered at the makeshift table. No etiquette or manners, just digging in and enjoying, except that Zia Ginnie was served in a very gentlemanly fashion by Andrea, Meri's only male grandchild. The beautiful roast peppers and eggplant set perfectly on my plastic plate. Everyone talked at once, arms stretched here and there, taking this and that, wine flowed like the Po. Andrea sat with the men and they discussed man things. The women and girls occupied the other end of the table and I sat in between trying to understand — the odd word or phrase jumping into my ears. When I thought I understood and attempted to make a contribution to the discussion with my ideas on how they should brush the dogs sometimes, howls of laughter erupted. It appeared they were discussing how they might prepare the meat next time. My inability to grasp the difference between "cane" (dog) and "carne" (meat) is understandable, given the close pronunciation of each word. I certainly did not mind the laughter — I have never made the same mistake again.

"Ah, Madonna", said Gloria, Andrea's sister, heaven forbid they barbecue her dogs.

Meri's youngest son, Georgio, is an avid hunter, and tossed his comment into the ring. "Why bother", he said, "cinghale, the local wild boar, tastes better than dog, way better". Poor Sara was devastated with the translation of this conversation, asking me if they really ate dogs. Sara always takes her pooch to bed with her and they snuggle like bugs in a rug for the night. Why bother indeed, I thought. Georgio's poor hunting dogs spend their lives on the end of chains, and have some leftover pasta and few scraps thrown out for them once a day. I could easily believe their meat would not be tasty and tender. I remembered being so angry upon discovery of how tight their collars were, the two-finger rule unknown or ignored. I tried to loosen them a notch but each collar was secured with a nut and bolt. As much as I tried to tell myself that this way of life is all the dogs know, it bothered me for ages. I will never agree with their treatment of animals as tools of work, deserving of no love and attention, but have learned to accept it as part of this way of life. I have always known I would make a terrible farmer.

It took two hours to wade through the feast, topped off with pastries and coffee. My backside felt like a square brick and it was time to make a move. Having started the ball rolling, everybody else got up and mucked in, helping to clean up and put stuff away. The pots were washed with water boiled on the stove and we rinsed them under the fontana springing from between some rocks.

Luigi and I decided to walk back down to Rovinaglia. Accompanied by Sara and three of Meri's grandchildren, Lorena, Gloria, and little Francesca, we set off into the forest of oak and chestnut with stops along the way to study big black dung beetles waddling across the path, and to rest and sip water. We passed several "maesta", votive pillars and little shrines dedicated to saints, and the Madonna. These are very common and can be seen along the country roads and hidden away in the forests miles from anywhere. The oldest ones are stone, others brick, newer ones of concrete blocks, not attractive but continuing an age-old tradition of prayer stops. What amazes me is that they are more often than not filled with fresh wild flowers or flowers from someone's garden. The bottle of water always standing to attention so one can top up the vase as one passes by.

The way down was far more beautiful than that awful trek in the jeep. There was time to notice the huge oak trees and wonderful canopy of chestnut trees from which the ladies still gathered chestnuts and ground them down for flour. The occasional views through odd openings among the trees to the hills in the distance, the tiny wild flowers snuggled in the rocks and grass beneath the trees. And oh, those aromatic Laburnum blooms dripping from the trees in yellow and white. Just too much! We had a great time with the kids and after such an enlightening and enjoyable get together, I really began to feel as though I belonged in this family.

The free and easy, relaxed atmosphere was very different from the stiff and uncomfortable family dinner we had had years ago when we visited Nona with the kids. The whole family had attended in Meri's dining room, seated round a huge table. Beautiful china, glasses, and silverware were set on a linen tablecloth, with napkins. It all seemed so out of place, it did not fit with their lifestyle. After the beautiful meal over which Meri had slaved all afternoon in a baking hot kitchen, I did not score any brownie points with Nona who regarded my manner with great scorn, when I refused to rush off to the kitchen with the women to do women's work while the men remained lolling in their chairs, smoking and drinking wine. My trying to rally the males to muck in and help caused varying looks of shock and horror and gagging laughter. Nothing has changed in the traditional village families where the women still toil away in the kitchen without the help of their men. I have never understood whether this "women do women's work" thing is an entrenched cultural tradition or the women go on like this because they truly enjoy being slaves to their men. Having come from a family where men did and still do dishes, cook and vacuum, and having a very domesticated husband, it is beyond me why any woman would want to wear herself out in the kitchen while the men sit around like useless lumps. In Meri's case it was doubly harsh because she worked hard on the farm and with the animals as well as providing total and complete care to her family. Now, with a grown daughter who is helpful at times and can exhibit tremendous disrespect for her mother at other times, making caustic, abrupt demands, often rude and argumentative, Meri still runs around catering to their every need. When these incidents occur in my presence, I have to leave because I know, if I blow it will be considered very inappropriate. One does not interfere in the upbringing of another mother's children.

We arrived in Rovinaglia just as the four-wheelers came tumbling down from Monte Pero. The kids mounted the various trucks and were gone before we knew it. Thankfully so—I found it very tiring trying to carry on continual conversation with kids in Italian.

A pleasant quiet evening was in store for us. Sara and I were treated to an old story about the witch's house up in the woods past Casa di Grossi. Giulio's family owned a fair amount of land up there and it was on this land that a strange family had decided to squat, taking over one of the old huts. The gossip was that they were witches. The kids would cross this creepy area to see the witch's house. The witch-kids were always locked in the house. When the parents left, Luigi and his friends could hear them screaming inside. As they ran across the clearing in front of the hut they would cross themselves hoping to ward off evil spirits. I think Luigi was very successful—he does not have an evil bone in his body. One day the witches disappeared, never to be seen again. Sara and I eyed each other secretly, we knew we would go looking for the witch house. She also wanted to camp overnight up at Genovese, in the trees. She wanted to observe the wild boars that come out at night, snuffling for mushrooms. We started making plans but the next day proved to be far too interesting to spend time on witches and wild boars.

It was August 14th, 1997, my son's birthday. What a day to remember! I am sure he was breathing in the fresh air of the Okanagan, hurtling down the bike trails. Mom and Dad were not so lucky. That morning, we awoke to a reeking odor which enveloped us, the house, and the whole world it seemed. On the occasional day, we had noticed an unpleasant waft here and there, depending on wind direction. Most septic tanks lids in Italy are at ground level, not buried in hell as ours was in Canada, so it is not uncommon to experience the exuberance of this smell. From mountain villages to the streets of Florence the odor will occasionally assault one's senses.

But this was powerful. Discovering that the tub and toilet were not draining and the smell was coming from the overflow vent of the bath, Luigi put on his plumber hat and ventured forth into unknown frontiers. Knee deep in shit would be an adequate description of where he found himself. The old septic tank had obviously done its thing for who knows how many years and was now tired and worn out at playing host to this sudden onslaught of our continued use of the "facilities".

Watching him wading around in the quagmire in Nona's old "wellies", I kept very quiet. His, and the locals', fear of snakes was very real. Over the years a number of villagers had succumbed to those two or three which are poisonous. Sara and I had heard a strange rustling a few weeks prior, below the bedroom window. At that time I looked out to see the writhing courtship of two huge snakes, black and yellow and tones of green. Not a fisherman's story, they were at least the diameter of my upper arm, length unknown but obviously quite long! This was right beside the septic tank that he was now excavating, but my theory is what the eye does not see, the heart does not grieve over. Hopefully they had moved on with all the disturbance, I was ready with my exacto knife and sucking abilities, just in case.

The sloping vegetable garden on the lower side of the house overlooking the valley had become a quagmire of "ick". I suppose Nona had never thought to put an envelope of Septonic or a handful of rotten meat down the loo to aid in the break down of solid waste, and of course neither had we.

Our septic tank experiences had been twenty years earlier in Prince George. We had forgotten they can only take so much abuse. We had no idea that the vegetable garden was the location of the septic tank, and field. As it had obviously been leaking for sometime, I was quite amazed that no one had contracted some ghastly virus or typhoid. Needless to say, we never ate anything from the garden ever again, and would not let Meri plant anything there.

Fortunately this inconvenience was occurring close to our departure time. Luigi spent a lot of time working in this open-air sewer, digging out around the tank, hauling rocks to improve the drainage field, and putting lots of devouring enzymes into the tank. He sealed the top preventing any odor from escaping and re-landscaped the whole area so that the top of the tank sat beneath about three feet of earth.

We knew that we would have to get a new tank put in if we intended on returning. The lane behind the house is only used by the few residents of Costa Dazi, we thought this would be the best location. The equipment would have access and room to dig the hole and install the tank and there would be space to install a new field. Although the lane is not part of the property belonging to the house, it is very common to see the circular concrete tops of septic tanks peeking through public thoroughfares. The wind roars down the lane like an express through a tunnel and flies out into the farmyard, so any escaping smell would blend nicely into those surroundings. Roberto agreed to do the work for us which would help to reduce the millions and millions of lire we could see this project costing.

With only a few days remaining before we had to head home and our lungs completely overwhelmed with the disgusting aroma we just had to get away for a day. We set off along the main road to Parma which follows the Taro valley between amazing rock formations and colored strata patterns streaking canyon walls. The river winds back and forth, deep dark pools, white rushing, bubbling water cascading across beds of shingle. At each bridge crossing, the road drops to the valley bottom and then climbs again where faded blue signs indicate the villages snuggled in the hills above. Always a church and the inevitable osteria close by, allowing the needs of the body and soul to be satisfied within steps of each other. Baselica, Belforte, Caffaraccia, Tiedoli, the names alone are enough to lure us ever upwards along narrow, snaking roads. Off the beaten track, the lack of tourists and commercialism attracts us most. There is always a feeling of humble sincerity in the air. It is not necessary to encounter humans to experience this sense, it is just there.

We headed up toward Mt. Molinatico, a naked, round-topped hill decorated with radio antennae, like a cake with candles. The road leads through several villages, and we stopped here and there doing the usual poking around for inscribed rocks and headstones, dates over old doors. We found a small church which was being renovated. Inside a stocky, shirt-sleeves-rolled-up man was working away in the dirt, attacking piles of rubble. But the altar, which stood bare and undecorated, was ready for business. I could not imagine how a congregation would care to kneel on rubble and inhale dusty incense, let alone sit on the few rickety old pews.

The workman, who in fact was the priest, proudly showed us around his church. He had undertaken the work himself, raised the money to fund the project because the Diocese could not or would not help. I thought it might be a good idea if our village priest was to roll up his shirt sleeves and get some dirt under those pious fingernails. It would do him good to undertake some physical labor. He might even be able to keep that middle button buttoned.

The outside of this lovely little church was restored to the original rock, the bell tower was quite lovely, not overpowering as they often are but a nice unobtrusive companion to the church. Beside the church was the priest's house and in the yard were chickens and ducks and some exotic, feathered fluffy duck things with red faces and fluffy pants.

The door of the house opened and out stepped a veritable bird of paradise. Quite in keeping with the odd looking birds now surrounding her, she was dressed in tight leopard-print leggings and a brightly colored shirt. The blackest, curly mop of hair was somewhat contained in an electric pink scarf wrapped around her head. Sister or housekeeper to the priest, who knows, but she was quite delighted to have visitors and pointed out how the wildflowers were to be found only in this area because of its unique natural features. Weeds are weeds, according to the farmers, I thought as I glanced at a pile of garden waste, but the wild flowers surrounding the area were truly glorious.

The church stood alone, with no village nearby. The cemetery up the hill was fully populated which seemed to indicate that a congregation once existed, and still must, as evidenced by the priest's successful fundraising.

Our idea had been to go up to Molinatico where Luigi, proudly displaying his new mushroom hunters' license, could legally forage for the great porcini. No more sneaking around in the undergrowth! We had driven up to Mt. Molinatico a few weeks prior to this day. Luigi had gone off mushrooming and I sat in the shade, drawing, among the wonderful beech trees with their gorgeous gnarled and twisted trunks, like lurking ghouls. The sun sparkled down through the little holes in the canopy of leaves. Before I knew it Luigi returned with lots of mushrooms. The porcini were huge and he also had what the villagers call "poor man's mushrooms". Different shapes and sizes and colors—oh the colors, there were blue and mauve and yellow and green and gold and creamy colors. Of course we would check with Meri before eating any. Luigi would not eat them anyway not being overly fond of mushrooms. All the more for me. I was already imagining a huge feast! Luigi told me how he had had his picnic lunch in the woods with a young man and his grandfather. The old man was eating a cheese that had live, wriggling maggots, "ibegi", in it. A delicacy, Luigi pointed out to me, his family used to eat when he was a kid. With churning stomach I contemplated anew my "mushroom feast". The first course of action on arriving home had been to slice the porcini and spread them out on wire racks to dry in the sun. I performed my most enjoyable little task until I had the strange experience of movement, as if the complete layers of porcini were on the move. As I looked closer I saw little wormy-things popping their heads out from the slices, even the ones I had sliced through were wriggling. It was so revolting! Just at that point Pierina popped over and discussed the day's harvest. I pointed at the wriggling mass of mushrooms and she laughed, explaining that the sun brings the worms out and they all die, the flavor and quality of the mushrooms are not affected, in fact they are enhanced. She is such a tease, I did not know whether to believe her or not but remembering Luigi's story about the ibegi in the old man's cheese, I was inclined to believe her. Meri was my trusted mushroom expert so off I went with a sample and the basket of poor man's mushrooms. She weeded out a few poisonous ones and said Pierina was right about the worms (which amazed me considering the animosity that exists between them). But she was disturbed that I was intending to have a huge mushroom feast. "Your liver, your liver" she cried "it's not good for your liver". Well I had my feast and I am still here. In fact when I returned to Canada my liver scan revealed a mighty reduction in the amount and sizes of the tumors. Perhaps hidden in the Emilian woods is the magic ibegi cure for liver lesions!

On this current trip, after the detours to look at the hillside churches and explore villages along the way, the mushroom hunt was given a rain check. It was too late in the day. Ardent hunters know that these elusive mushrooms peak between the hours of five and mid-morning, it was now almost noon. We continued on, just for the lovely ride. The vegetation and strata were changing imperceptibly with the elevation. Lush growths of chestnut dwindled as we climbed into the realm of the evergreens. When we broke out into a completely barren wasteland of moulded volcanic lava fields we knew we had taken the wrong road. Molinatico is clothed with forests except for its rounded topknot, which is quite bare. The road became narrower and rockier, with obvious watercourses scoring the surface. Luigi ever the intrepid explorer forged even higher as I whimpered like a sniveling coward. Bumping and spinning our way along we arrived suddenly at what seemed, to me at least, Valhalla. A beautiful house set in an oasis of trees and lush growth, flowers blooming everywhere. A monstrous great teddy of a dog gamboled across our path and romped round and round the car. We pulled up beside the gate and a rather ancient looking old fellow came forward to retrieve the dog. I do not know what prompted my crazy husband to ask, "What's for lunch?" but the man threw up his hands in delight and demanded that we stay and visit and thus began another of those chance encounters at which we seem to be so good. An equally frail old lady appeared and together they insisted on giving us a tour of their property. Leading us round to the back of the house, they proudly showed off their efforts. Half the property stretched up the hill through the trees; they had created a huge natural rock garden and we were led up and down and round and along the winding path through the rockery. We inspected every flowering shrub that she had planted and nurtured. I especially loved the lavender bushes. Always a favorite of mine, I stroked the aromatic leaves and swooned as I held my hands to my face to inhale. We were shown round the gorgeous old house and introduced to the children and grandchildren, framed and proudly displayed on one wall.

There were a number of original paintings to which I was attracted and in showing my interest I inadvertently fell into a delightful discovery. Hauled away by the old man, I was taken to his studio, a small separate building, designed and built by himself, in perfect harmony with the old house. The studio was simple, containing the basic necessary elements that he needed to work in oils. I thought how trusting they were of two complete strangers as they chatted about their lives here in the summer and back in Milan during the winter. They had chosen this isolated spot as a refuge to get away from everyone and everything, although it was quite obvious they were more than happy to have at least a little human contact. They told us that the road improved further up and the views over the steep lava beds were worth experiencing. We left, without lunch, much to my relief, ever embarrassed by my silly husband, and crept onwards and upwards to the view. The little twosome and the huge dog stood at the gate watching until we were out of sight.

We spent another hour marveling at the black tumbling mounds and formations shoved out of the earth millions of years ago, and then set out back down the road. As we neared the house the old lady stood at the gate and waved us down. She presented me with several plants of rooted lavender and I was very taken with her thoughtfulness. The fragrance flooded through the car. Those three little roots have become beautiful bushes in my garden in Rovinaglia. Never a day passes there where I do not draw my hands up through the leaves and flowers and inhale, getting lavender brain. I could absolutely overdose on the fragrance. It is a sensation that takes me back in time to my childhood, to our beautiful garden in England and the lavender lined paths.

For all the beauty of the lavender, reality awaited as we made our way home. A quick paddle in the river and time to eat our cheese buns and then returning home to a still sleeping Sara. By this time we had given up hounding Sara about her schoolwork. A month of digging her out of her bear's den at two o'clock and trying to get her to mail her work to Canada on time was not worth the stress. Luigi, as usual, prepared a wonderful dinner. It was now nearly six o'clock and Sara had not appeared. I peeped in her room and just at that moment I heard her voice. She had been out all day exploring with Gloria.

The next day we thought a cultural trip to Modena might be interesting for Sara. She had not visited a bigger city and besides, the International Garden and Horticulture Exhibit was taking place in Modena. It had rained the day before in Modena and the mud was quite thick and deep in places.

Sara tramped from exhibit to exhibit along the muddiest route she could find. By the time we left her shoes and jeans legs were covered in mud. She became very bored so we decided to drive into the heart of Modena to wander round and enjoy this beautiful city with its arcaded streets and many historical sites. Beautiful palazzos stood sedately behind huge iron gates and massive, thick wooden studded doors, churches, gardens, and ancient piazzas all awaited us.

It would have been most irresponsible of us to leave a thirteen year old Canadian girl in a car in Italy but Sara did not want to join us on our walk. We were all tired and the heat was oppressive out of the shade, but we really wanted to give her the opportunity to enjoy another side of Italian life, so different from village life. She objected steadfastly with arms folded tight, mouth pouting. She simply refused to leave the car. From somewhere in the depths of my English soul leapt the fish-wife. As Sara continued to object, I took her arm and yanked her from the car in the most unladylike manner, yelling some awful expletives within hearing of all the beautiful people as they floated by in their Gucci shoes and Versace suits. Perhaps I had not behaved as a lady should but strong-arm tactics was the only resort. Mission accomplished, we soothed our three troubled selves with gelati and cappuccini and little pastry things. With blood pressures at a safe level, we left the sidewalk café and its colorful umbrellas, beginning our walk through the city.

We found the most beautiful, calming place of the day. Walking beneath a huge archway between massive iron gates we discovered a wonderful arcaded courtyard. A single purple wisteria, dripping with blossoms, had branched from one huge trunk and perhaps a hundred or two hundred years ago began its adventurous climb round the arcades in both directions. The vines were now within inches of meeting on the wall opposite the trunk. What history the beautiful wisteria must have grown through. Which dukes and contessas had inhaled its fragrant aroma? What battles and wars had it survived? Surely it must have given inspiration to minds, to create, to compose, to paint. We left this gorgeous haven and continued on along cobbled streets, past churches and surrounding centuries old buildings, wide piazzas, umbrella-covered tables outside the cafes hosting their coffee drinkers, plates of proscuitto and parmesan to entice the senses. Buon appetito!

An amusing moment arose as we walked through a park and Luigi, out of the blue as usual, asked a lady seated on a park bench if she knew Modena's most famous tenor. As Sara and I cringed, the lady in a gleeful manner began to relate the poor man's life history. Of course she knew him, his wife, his girlfriend, and where he lived and everything else about the man we might want to know. We probably could have read about this poor chap's love life in the National Enquirer. Given the choice, I would rather be in a beautiful park in Modena as I learned the details.

After completing our walk through Modena we sat once more at shaded tables with cool drinks, and talked about what we had seen and done, and agreed it had been a good day. Sara appeared to have enjoyed the experience but remained tight-lipped towards me. The atmosphere in the car driving home could have been cut with a knife. It was difficult at least to me, not having dealt with teenagers for so long. During our final few days, Sara began to perk up. She was very eager to get home.

On the last morning as we locked the door behind us I wondered what the future held. Would we ever use that key again?

The greetings between Sara and her mom, in Canada, were emotional. It made me realize that all our trials and tribulations with this young lady came to naught in the faces of love, as mom and child hugged and wept and laughed. I will always remember Sara's remark to her mom, that Rovinaglia is a place that time has forgotten.

CHAPTER IV

1998

The fall was no different this year in Canada, a beautiful time in the Okanagan Valley. The clear air seems to magnify the brilliance of the colors. We are blessed with a variety of deciduous trees, a wonderful array of yellows, oranges and browns set against the blue, blue lakes and sprinkled among the fir trees. Above the lakes, parks and gardens, and the tree-lined avenues, are the vineyards and orchards. Their fertile carpets reach up to the dry hills, home to stretches of waving grassland and sagebrush, quail and grouse, and rattlesnakes hidden in the heat of the rocks. Much of this land forms part of the reserve land belonging to the Okanagan Indian tribe whose horses wander freely through the hills. Higher up are the Ponderosa Pines, those wondrous giants, sending roots far beneath the surface in search of underground waters, evolved to exist in these arid surroundings. Their huge roots are often exposed, as they cling to rocky crags. The surrounding hills continue to rise, home to thicker growths of fir and pine. These hills are home to deer, coyotes, big horn sheep, black bears, and the cougars, which range even higher. All this surrounds me, how can I be so fortunate to live my life in two of the most beautiful places on earth?

The winter usually wanders in slowly, frosty mornings, a little snow here and there, sometimes chilly north winds. Occasionally, with little warning, it arrives abruptly with swirling white storms and freezing temperatures. The lakes turn to pearl and slate, purple and indigo as the skies take on their winter colors. Clouds hang in a thick blanket above the

valley. We will not see much blue sky until February, however, just a short drive takes us up and out of the closed in
atmosphere to sparkling snow clad trees and hills reaching
on to the mountains, bright sun and blue skies.

When I am tucked up inside my warm Canadian house, I
often wonder about Rovinaglia, a bleak and unforgiving place
in the winter. Howling ferocious winds, snow storms severe
enough to isolate the villages high on the hillsides. As much
as I love Rovinaglia, I have no desire to be there in the winter. I contemplate the endurance of the villagers. I know they
will be sitting hunched round the wood stoves, scarves
wrapped round sore throats and hot poultices on wheezing
chests, rheumatic joints, and bodies ravaged by every virus
known to man. They will have lots to complain about, a staple
of life to support them through another winter.

I will think of Nona too. Of her years spent in the small
house. Winters of cold, damp misery, freezing pipes, with
only the faithful old Aga to keep her warm. She would hang
thick curtains over all the windows, close off the other rooms
and exist in the kitchen, sleeping on the old wooden bench.
Her dishes, her clothes, and herself were washed in the
cracked porcelain kitchen sink, with only one cold water tap
and the Aga to heat pots of water. In earlier years, without
the benefit of a decent bathroom, she would struggle through
the snow and rain and freezing winds to the outhouse. What
a tough old bird! I could see where her son's rock-hard determination came from.

Our winters here in the Okanagan are at least more toler-
able, even comfortable, when compared to the old stone
house. Time passes quickly, chemo treatments come and go
and before we know it the daffodils are blooming and the
buds are spurting, the birds are screaming their heads off
and the cats are going bananas.

My request for a good break from chemo was granted. The
oncologist agreed that six weeks would be safe. Long enough
to enjoy a good rest and short enough to act should things go

awry. We were disappointed that the discussions over Nona's land were still dragging on, hoping by now we would have been notified of pending finalization. Nevertheless our desire was still strong to visit Rovinaglia and we hoped I would be healthy and the RRSP's would perform well. We spent hours talking about how we could improve the area round the house. There were changes we could make inside without undertaking any physical reconstruction or restoration. Besides, my addiction to the historical and cultural aspects of Emilia Romagna could never be satisfied no matter how many times we traveled there. It only felt like a blink of an eye as, with the necessary arrangements in place, we ventured forth once again with renewed energy and the never failing excitement and anticipation of being in our little piece of Italy.

After sailing through customs in Munich and completing paperwork for the rental car, we set out to find our steed. With a bike in a box, a bike-rack in a box, two huge suitcases on wheels and various bags stuffed with far more than we would ever need, with art stuff which was far more important to me than clothes, we approached the smallest car on the lot. We stuffed the little car full, stuck the rack on the back and the bike on the rack and headed south.

Germany was an unknown quantity to us. I had spent the first four years of my life in Northern Germany with my parents and brother and sister. Fleeting memories of our house and some toys, a duck doing poo in my cot, placed there by my silly father, were all that remained. The fact that my first language had been German because I had spent most of the days of those four years with my German nanny, was not helpful to me now. The language could have been Chinese. With the phrase book conveniently packed deep in the bowels of a bag somewhere in the car, we struggled through our requests for a room and breakfast at a lovely little hotel about an hour out of Munich.

Paranoid about theft, we dragged everything up three

flights of stairs, bike and rack included. We were rewarded with a gorgeous room, soft, pillowy duvets and piles of fresh white towels in the sparkling bathroom. A huge sloping floor-to-ceiling window revealed a not spectacular view, but pleasant, across roof tops and trees.

After the long journey cramped on the plane and the subsequent hour of driving stuffed in the tiny car, space, fresh air and exercise was what we needed. We went for a walk and saw some sign and arrows indicating biking paths and footpaths. We set out along one of these, which crossed the autobahn. The power and speed of the machinery hurtling beneath us was incredible. The vibration coming through the surface of the bridge felt like a foot massage. Crossing the bridge we saw a sign with the word "zee" preceded by a name. I remembered that we had been in a little sailboat on a lake when I was a toddler and knew that zee must be some kind of lake or pond. We discovered a beautiful, almost circular lake rimmed with a treed grassy area and the footpath. It took us an hour to walk round this peaceful place. Fishermen sat on the shore, their lines dangling in anticipation. Dogs ran and kids played, we could have stayed for the rest of the evening but tomorrow's lengthy drive loomed so we headed back to the hotel.

The next morning we found a lovely breakfast room with a stupendous array of cheeses and sliced meats, yogurts, cereals both hot and cold, boiled eggs, toast, and different jams, several different real juices. A hot china pot of the best coffee in Germany was on our table. I wished that my stomach was on European time so I could enjoy this huge feast but I was still at ten o'clock at night. I downed a bit of sustenance and drank all the coffee. We left at eight o'clock. Southern Germany was beautiful. Austria and Switzerland likewise, but we did not allow ourselves to stop too often because we had decided to make the return trip over three days and enjoy these beautiful places in a more leisurely fashion. Ten hours later, we arrived in Rovinaglia, driving down the slope in front of the old barn and parking with sighs of relief.

Without realizing, we must have communicated to some-one in the family our feelings about arriving in the past to a dark, cold, powerless house. The place was sparkling. On the kitchen table stood a vase containing a huge bouquet of flowers and a card written by Gloria. The towels, the linen, the clothes we had left behind last year, were freshly laun-dered and pressed. Chairs and cushions were set out, de-moth-balled, plump and inviting. We had no doubt that Gloria and her mom, Anna, her aunty Rosetta and cousin Lorena were responsible. What a welcome to be sure.

The morning brought the breathtaking view, the bells, the sun, and our neighbor, Marietta down in her garden work-ing away, digging and weeding, communing with nature. It also brought Meri. Firing on all eight cylinders, she was primed and ready for battle. A nice smile and hug for me, a withering welcome for her brother.

"We're having a family meeting at ten, be there"!

"We have to go to town for groceries", said Luigi calmly.

"Just make sure you're back in time", she said and left abruptly. How he manages to remain relatively level in his emotions over all the haggling I do not know.

We rushed off to buy food, noticing how much more ex-pensive it had become since our last visit (try with a good conscience to buy two bananas for four dollars, impossible). Home we rushed, the fridge and cupboards were once again re-stocked. Off we tore to squeeze under the ten o'clock dead-line imposed by Madam Chairwoman, but no one was in the garage. Giulio was meandering across the farmyard and then exploding out of the house came Meri. Everything seemed to part like Moses dividing the Red Sea. Dogs went one way, cats another, Pierina who had been walking up the hill, turned and walked back down, Giulio spun like a teetering old man and just managed to make his bench before collapsing. I was enjoying it all but Luigi was less than thrilled. Nothing much was accomplished in the hour that followed except that Luigi made it clear he wanted Banshoele and Genovese. There was a little plus, Meri was willing to give us about half an acre just down the hill. Back to the house we went, waving sweet goodbyes, as smoke came out of Luigi's ears. He prepared a quick lunch, we were eager to get over to Genovese and see what ten months of neglect had done.

The undergrowth was thick and almost impenetrable. Thorns and brambles grabbed our legs and ripped at our arms. Luigi forged ahead hacking away and we made a path through to the highest part of Genovese. Sitting at the edge of Genovese and looking out over the meadows stretching up and over the surrounding hills, we once again marveled at the view, the feelings for this gorgeous place still so strong.

❧ ❧ ❧

Regardless of the fact that we still held no legal ownership, I considered Genovese to be my piece of land and the trees upon it mine. They also had grown into a thick forest. By selective thinning, pruning, and cutting we could improve this piece of land thereby adding to the beauty of the surrounding area. Our reasoning will not wash with the Polizia Forestale. A license is necessary (another mile of red tape and thousands of lire into the coffers) to cut trees and then only at selected times of the year. We wanted to construct a grape arbor on the piazza at the house. The chestnut trees grow so profusely it would be possible to sneak some off Genovese.

As Luigi hacked his way through the undergrowth I stood guard, watching the gravel road that runs smack bang through the middle of Genovese. The longer Luigi remains in Rovinaglia the more like the villagers he becomes. He is furious about this road, made by a man who lives about another three kilometers along. This fellow just took it upon himself to bulldoze the road for easier access to his house. I know Luigi wants to put up barriers but he never will. He will calm down eventually. Genovese is not ours, it is very frustrating, we just want to let our hair down and get on with the work. But so far so good, that dreaded green forestry Land Rover camouflaged deliberately, to catch the poor unfortunate peasants was nowhere to be seen. Oh yes, feeling suitably guilty but insistent upon my "rights", I would slot right into the Sunday griping session outside the church, just like an old hand.

Risking the three hundred dollar fine, we rattled our way back up the road at an agonizingly slow pace. Our trusty little rental car was laden with poles hanging from the hatchback to make our grape arbor. What did the rental agreement say? No off-road driving, yes, but I did not read anything about loading the car down until the tires rubbed against the wheel wells. I sweated and trembled like a fool the whole way back to the house. I have never been very good at being dishonest. Even when I am guilty of nothing I quiver as the eyes of authority bore through my soul. Given the third degree whenever returning to Canada, I tremble and blush. The most I ever "smuggle" is a piece of parmesan and some dried porcini. For what I put myself through it might as well be a bag full of drugs.

It was only after we had dragged the poles round the corner of the house and out of sight of the road that I noticed the dreaded green devil passing by on the top road. The silly side of this caper being that I would allow myself to be drawn into several more "pole heisting" escapades. I really cannot imagine why I felt so like a thief because Luigi can talk his way out of anything. Even if he could not, what was the worst that could happen? About five years down the road, we would have to fork over three hundred dollars, after all, we knew the legal wheels turned mighty slowly in this part of the world.

The holes for the poles were dug, no easy task, through chunks of rock the size of boxes. Poles in, cement poured, cross beams attached, and we were ready for the vines. Grapes, Virgina creeper, Old Man's Beard, anything that would grow fast, provide shade and a modicum of privacy. Another pole heisting trip was necessary to get poles for a small grape vine support down the hill on the half acre that Meri had reluctantly agreed to give to Luigi.

I leaned out the window to see what Luigi was up to. He was heading down the hill to our measly half-acre to "release" his grandfather's one surviving grape which over the years had been mowed down, choked with hay, eaten by cows, and assaulted by who knew what other ugly fates. He had a special attachment to this vine because it was one of a whole vineyard that existed when he was a boy and he remembers helping tend his grandfather's vines, spending hours among the rows stretched down the hillside on the rock terraces.

As Luigi lugged the poles down the hill to build the arbor for the grapevine to climb, he was watched by three older and wiser men, Giulio, Pepino, and cousin Bruno. They have that certain way of looking, transmitting their message silently but surely. Giulio had already said Luigi was wasting his time attempting to resurrect the dead-as-a-doornail root. And I could see from their body language that they were thinking "daft Canadian does not know what he is doing, no sense. Oh, these people from the new-world, no idea, no idea at all". As usual, their negativity and doubt drove him on to succeed.

Slowly the arbor took shape and from our window view the three posts each with a cross pole just drove me to sing "There is a Green Hill Faraway". Luigi shouted up to the old guys, "One for each of you, you old reprobates." I pressed on with my hymn. The noise and scoffing laughter from the men brought out the old biddies who twittered like hens. For once there was much merriment. Pierina was nowhere to be seen. I thought she might be hiding in the woodshed, frantically crossing herself and praying for Luigi's redemption. As usual, Luigi would triumph in the face of adversity. Next year the vine would produce sixteen bunches of tiny grapes, hanging like green opalescent gems, from the vine which has crawled all over the arbor.

Bless his heart, my dear husband who is always full of new and exciting ideas, suggested I make a basket with strips of bark he had peeled away from the poles. I had hinted many times that I wanted Giulio to apply his well known weaving talents to make me a basket and restring the old chairs, but he had not to this point. With nothing to lose I selected strips of similar widths and lengths. My idea was pretty basic. Lie eight strips across another eight. Weave a center square about 24" x 24". Fold the unwoven ends up and take more strips to weave round and round to build up the sides. This was great fun. It was looking better all the time. I spent about two hours alternately on my knees and bent double and at times needing eight arms to control the lively strips of bark with minds of their own. I devised a way to finish the rim by bending the strips over and weaving them back down the sides. I had been bent double for so long I was unable to get up and thought I looked like Marietta with her crooked old back, but I had made a bloody good basket.

Luigi, always one to boast about the merits of his family must have sent out smoke signals. As my basket sat in the sun to dry it was visited by everyone I knew and even some that I did not. I cringed behind the shutters. What would they think? They must be having a good laugh at my expense. When the best basket maker in the whole wide world limped round on his new stainless steel hip to view this pathetic thing, I wanted to fall through a hole in the floor and disappear forever. There he stood, Giulio with Luigi, discussing no doubt my lack of basket making skills. Oh, come on Virginia, I told myself, go out there and be proud of your handiwork. You think it is good. You like it. Since when did you care what other people think of you? And so I did, and discovered in fact that he and everyone else it seemed thought Ginnie's basket was okay. Better than they could do said some of the old ladies.

The villagers, as always, wandered by along the top road

casting surreptitious glances. Our arbor was obviously causing a stir. "Bongiorno", I shouted, getting a little satisfaction
from catching them in the act of spying. "Ciao Signora," they
called, their stiff waves and tight smiles belying their acute
embarrassment at being caught out. The English blood flowing through my veins demands privacy. I could not wait to
get my vines, to prune, to fertilize. I would even talk to them,
just grow, please grow. Give me some privacy is all I ask!
For the time being I had to be content with a line of washing.
Strategically hung, it blocks the view into our piazza from
the top road. I learned never to hang out the washing on a
Sunday. It appeared if one had time to do laundry one had
time to go to church.

Eventually I would overcome my insular English ways and
enjoy the natural curiosity of these people. We certainly did
not have to invent ways to incur their interest in our lives.
Whether I painted or sunbathed, potted plants or swept the
patio there was always a stray villager on that top road. Any
rockwork or tree trimming or cement pouring was scruti-
nized from afar, I am sure for its correctness and perfection.

We bought our vines the next day and then set off again in
our all-purpose Fiat, heading for "Cow Bruno's" farm to get
manure. With buckets, boots, shovels and bags, we assaulted
the mountain of cow dung. Entering the realm of the voracious, massive horseflies, we feared for our lives as we
shoveled and loaded as fast as we could. Oh God, the smell
was disgusting. This huge, wreaking pile of muck was steam-
ing. Almost overcome by the fumes, I looked up to see "Cow
Bruno" perched on his tractor. His grin stretched from ear to
ear, revealing many gaps among his few remaining tobacco
stained teeth, his eyes twinkling, his amusement evident as
he laughed aloud at the spectacle before him.

He is the last holdout up here of the livestock generation.
Every day of every month of every year, he herds his magnificent stock of fifteen great milking cows out of the barn
and across the road. Leaving their plops of smelly evidence

they wander down the lane heading for the meadows. They will graze happily until four o'clock at which time they will begin to head home. "Cow Bruno" rests awhile, leaning on his staff, hands crossed cushioning his chin. Lost in thought, his cows, his life, he turns to guide them back, or do they guide him? A time of union and peace between animal and man. Again the plops across the road, the earlier mounds run flat with imprints of tire treads. Those same tires now parked outside Meri's house or downtown in the piazza, permeating the cappuccino, blending with the incense wafting from the church. Giuliana is quite convinced that Cow Bruno deliberately drives his animals across the road just before she heads down to work at seven and home again at four. Running the gauntlet every day, flying around the winding curves at breakneck speed but always getting caught on the wrong side of the manure trail, this elegant young lady becomes a screaming, thrashing fishwife. Leaping out of her car, arms flying, thumb tip to fingertips, hand raised revealing her total contempt for Bruno and his stinking cows. "Quelle vacche e la strada tuti sporche di merda", she screams. "Those cows and the street full of filthy shit. He has never liked me, he is jealous because his old woman looks like a shoe". We listened and tried not to laugh while Luigi made helpful suggestions such as comparing Giuliana to a wild animal, that we could sell tickets to the spectacle and make money exhibiting this fiery she-cat. As the ranting beauty stomped off into the house she gave Luigi a withering look and did not speak to him again for the duration of our stay. Did we really want Giuliana, this young Italian hellion, to visit us in Canada? I have worked with high school and college students, Luigi has taught young apprentices but I at least, do not recall encountering such a volatile personality in a young lady. I was once pinned to the wall by a big grade twelve boy but even that experience did not seem as bad as Giuliana's reaction. It felt like a slap in the face.

What a variety of personalities this little village has

spawned.

Giuliana, a thrashing young beauty locked into a life full of old, bitter people. Wanting to escape but unable, for who knows what reason lacking the ability to make such a move.

"Cow Bruno", content with his lot. A peaceful uncomplicated life, shoveling cow dung, milking at five o'clock in the morning, cutting firewood, mending fences, raking hay, milking at six o'clock in the evening. There is an unorganized comfort in his house with the warped green shutters at the windows, rusting hinges, and the smell of cheese and baking bread as his "old shoe" of a woman takes care of the inside stuff.

A cousin, Lena, one of the five who had left Rovinaglia years ago as a child with her family to start a new life in Scotland. This was only the first move in her life, here began an odyssey of world travel, England, America, Australia, somehow finding time to have three children but never finding that special something she sought. Finally at seventy-six, she is settled in Australia with one daughter and son and her grandchildren.

And yet another woman fleeing the poverty and degradation for England, working her fingers to the bone in search of something, flailing around at the bottom of the ladder, seeking membership in "The Cut Above", striving to find security in materialism. Having apparently attained that life-long desire, she wallows in her life of perfection and wealth, among society's best known. "Lord so-an-so lives down there and that famous radio announcer lives around the corner. Oh yes, and I had tea with the wife of a Harley Street physician who has a patient who knows the lady-in-waiting to the Queen, you know. And did I tell you that my perfect, darling little six-week-old grandson is enrolled in Saint Someone's Academy from which he will graduate and go to Oxford." Yes, you have told me, over and over again.

There is the "Scott's Porridge Oats" lady, Katerina, when I remember her name among the Adelinas and the Natalinas, her Scottish brogue still so strong. She returned to the fold from Scotland years ago after being carted away with her brother to the Scottish Highlands. As adults she and her brother returned and she is content now to while her time away in the fields. Alone since her brother died and never having married, she spices her life with the church, the market and the odd trip to Lourdes or Rome.

Some continue their struggle to sever the ties to this village way of life, others are content to see it through to the inevitable conclusion, some complaining, some not.

A stroll through the villages that are Rovinaglia is always an interesting experience. The views, the personalities, the houses, even the fat duck that waddles in the ditch in Giacopazzi, all contribute to my enjoyment of this way of life. One road connects the separate little villages. Old cart trails lead off in different directions. One of these heads up the hill and just at the brow divides, where one branch goes off up past the "Sad Lady's" and "Tractor Boy's" house and on into the mountains. The other trail passes behind the "Dog Man's" house and then down into Giacopazzi.

The "Dog Man" and his wife and little girl are somewhat of an incongruity among the local inhabitants. Obviously wealthy and educated but not in any way flaunting those facts, they are very down to earth and work hard digging, planting and gathering the vegetables. He breeds and shows Italian hunting dogs and treats them like his children. He is so devoted to them that he has trouble parting with the puppies and will sometimes keep one or two. I think the dog population up there is now in the region of fifteen or so. His wife, having spent many years in London speaks perfect English. She devotes her time to their daughter and to her parents who recently retired from London to live in Casa di Grossi. She is terrified of anything with feathers. I was walking by one day when all their chickens were out on the road. As I looked up she had just come out onto the balcony. "Do you know your chickens are running free?" I called over the cacophony of the barking dogs. "Yes", she wailed, "but I am terrified of them. They'll have to stay out until my husband comes home". With visions of flattened feathered corpses on the road and eagles flying away with white bodies clutched in their talons, I offered to "herd" them back to safety. As her six year old daughter held the gate open I whistled and called in my most professional chicken herding manner and managed to steer all thirty of them through the gate into the field. The little girl shut the gate behind them and we looked proudly up at Mom as though we had achieved the impossible. I guess it was much more of an achievement than I realized.

My herding talent became the talk of the village. The word probably being spread by "Popeye", an old lady who does not miss a thing, who knows everything about everybody. I once saw her walking towards me some way off, which gave me the time to walk up the steep lane behind the "Dog Man's" house and avoid her. My evasive tactics were not successful. She lay in wait at the top of the hill having seen me slinking the other way. I was trapped in her gossip session for half an hour. She speaks English as she and her family had spent years in London. When my brother, Christopher visited Rovinaglia a huge coincidence was uncovered. While he was chatting with her husband, he discovered that the old man ran a café in the same area where Christopher plodded the streets as a London Bobby and would often drop into that same café for a good cup of tea.

I did discover some interesting aspects of Luigi's childhood and the lives of the kids who were his buddies. "Popeye" told me about Luigi's father, Lorenzo. How the kids loved him because he was so kind to them. During the winter on their way to school he would have hot drinks ready for them when they called for Luigi. He would see that their shoes were warmed up by the fire, then send them on their way to school. This was a side to Lorenzo about which I knew nothing. He made shoes out of old tires for the kids who had none, and wooden ski sets so the kids could have some fun in the winter. Much of the time the children were worked hard on the farms and on inside chores. The strap was a great inducement to obey and stay on the right track, and Lorenzo did not hesitate to target Luigi's bottom when he felt it necessary. "Popeye" certainly opened my eyes! Luigi's more recent teenage recollections from New York were tales of constant bitterness between his parents, disagreement and arguments rampant in their home. I can only imagine how miserable it must have been, how this part of his life had overshadowed the happier moments of childhood.

My favorite house is just up the road from the chicken place, among the group of houses called Giacopazzi. Very old, its walls exhibit patches of brick and rock where the crumbling ochre colored stucco has fallen away. Worn, warped bright blue shutters hang precariously at the windows and a tangled mass of climbing red roses have crept up and across the walls. During what must have been a sixty or seventy year journey they have traveled up to the eaves and into the eaves troughs and now venture forth across the terra cotta roof. Hanging in the doorway is an old, faded orange fly curtain made of long fuzzy strips of material. The occasional wave from a breeze is the only indication of movement at this house. Seldom seen are its occupants except for the old grandpa who perches on his favorite rock at the end of the house in the shade. His mind now departed to another plane, he sings away to himself in what seems to be unintelligible gibberish. The old dog and cat often lie at his feet. I will always turn and look back at the house from a higher point up the road beside the fat duck that is usually waddling in the ditch. The colors are what attract me most about this house. One does not often see blue shutters in this part of the world. Set against the crumbling old ochre walls, they leap out in happiness from among the gorgeous red roses. I might feel sadness at the spectacle of this old man on his rock if he was against the more usual background of drab gray stucco so common now, but I can only smile when I see him seated against this lovely, colorful old place. I always converse with the old fat duck and she looks at me, her head cocked just to one side and then to the other, believing I am sure, that this thing before her is an alien. People round here just do not talk to ducks, except of course for the old grandpa who will sing to her when she waddles by.

My usual route will take me on up the hill to the cemetery and church. Along the way I stop often to look out over the valley. The land drops away steeply and I can see over the tops of the beautiful chestnut trees covering the hillside. Because the church stands at an isolated spot and not in the middle of the group of homes it is kept locked, otherwise I would spend time looking round inside.

I have not seen the interior for a few years at which time it was badly in need of repair and maintenance. I cannot often be talked into attending a church service, or mass, but on one occasion I allowed Luigi to twist my arm. It was the yearly feast of Madonna del Carmine. Pierina will raid the flower gardens the day before gathering flower heads so that she can strew petals along the processional route through the village. I am very protective of our roses now. On that day when I looked out of the window to see Nona's roses picked clean, I was not pleased. I know Nona would have approved but she was tending a higher garden now. These roses were under my care. For want of better words, hands off my roses!

The procession was a lovely experience, despite shuffling through my rose petals. The whole congregation followed the priest and choir, everybody singing, a great feeling of communal happiness and harmony. The Madonna joggling along on her stand, proudly carried by four village men, down the aisle and out into the sun. To the furthest village she went, prayers and blessings, and then the up-hill, down-dale walk back to the church, more prayers and blessings and now safely tucked into her church for another year.

PRIEST'S WINDOW · FERRARI

Down the hill past the church sits Casa di Grossi, the larg-est cluster of houses gathered round what once was the osteria, a traditional bar and café where villagers would gather. When the old men talk about it, they always express sadness at the fact that it is now an ordinary house. The feel-ings of communal spirit exude from these places, common to most Italian villages, as people gather for a drink, card games, or just to talk. But those days are gone in Rovinaglia. The ever widening rift between the separate little clutches of houses, caused in part by the lack of this central meeting place, manifests itself in negative gossip, lack of caring or knowledge about each clutch of cottages and its inhabitants. If there is any connecting or caring between people from the various villages it appears between the elderly women as they wander through the village, they will sometimes gather in knots, arms will be placed around shoulders, in comfort. But gossip still abounds.

Luigi's good old friend the "Cat Lady" has become the latest target with some suggesting she and her husband only care for her senile old aunt because of the extra money they receive from the government. Luigi gets quite annoyed because he knows her so well and says her heart is huge. When they were children, he and his family and the "Cat Lady" and her family would spend the summers up at Monte Pero, driving the livestock up to the high meadows. These times were a highlight in Luigi's childhood. He hated school and the summer holidays gave more freedom. The families planted crops, barley, rye, root crops and maize. And even though it was a time for work there was still time for the kids to play and have fun and make lifetime bonds. The "Cat Lady" lives in Casa di Grossi, her house fronting the road presents a fresh white face to the world. The rock cornerstones are exposed revealing a time long gone when these houses were built. The windows are framed in fresh green shutters with geraniums dripping from their sills.

We often encounter her on our walks and she will invite us in for tea. Occasionally we accept. Dressed in her worn leather ankle boots, an old straight skirt to the knees covered with an apron, and wielding the ever present hiking stick, she leads the way through the arched tunnel toward the rear of the house. Here begins a journey into the past. Set into the walls of the tunnel are little grilled windows, small openings with ramps leading up to them, and old saucers and bowls for scraps. Every stray cat is welcomed here, hence my nickname for her. I can never remember whether she is Adelina, Natalina, or Katerina. They are three individual women but I cannot for the life of me remember who is who. The narrow concrete lane beneath the archway is littered with chicken scratch, bird droppings, and old tin plates and pans with the remains of animals' food. Chickens come and go at will and pigeons swoop in for any leftover seeds. The tunnel, about fifteen feet long and not quite wide enough to allow a small car, opens into a tattered old grass and weed covered, rocky courtyard. Various barns and sheds abut the yard, one of which displays a crusaders' cross in a rock set into the wall. The cross is surrounded by characters impossible to decipher by the layperson. These small buildings are full to bursting with old baskets, barrels, tools and farm implements. Parts of roofs have caved in and tiles and beams lie amongst the piles of junk. Negotiating a path between the cats and chickens takes us to the back door and into the kitchen. It is safer to enter with the "Cat Lady", who offers protection against the small black dog with lips curled back revealing white fangs and sharp little teeth. Growls and vicious sounding barks demand that we stay back. One command from her owner sends the little dog to the corner of the kitchen where she sits primed and ready to rip out throats. The kitchen must have been this way since her grandfather built the house. The inevitable wood stove is the centerpiece around which is gathered a sparse array of items essential to life in a kitchen. An old sideboard sits against the smoky sooty walls. Hanging above the stove are three wooden chestnut poles supported by bits of string attached to hooks screwed onto the grimy black beams. Odd items of clothing hang on the poles to dry. The inevitable rods stick out from the tin chimney, draped with washed clothes. Racks holding old pots and pans, ladles and tongs and kitchen implements are screwed to the walls. The tea-leaves are brewing in a saucepan of boiling water, guaranteed to be as thick as mud. Beautiful delicate bone china cups, at odds with the surroundings, are set on the plastic tablecloth covering the ancient table littered with crumbs and other food debris, as is the concrete floor where the cats rummage for scraps.

Propped up on a bench in the corner of the old kitchen is Julia. Ninety-eight years of living wrapped in a tiny bent frame of skin and bone. In a world of her own, she no longer communicates but her face is constantly graced with a smile. She lives here with her niece, the "Cat Lady", who takes care of her, as she is now completely immobile. I see love and that inborn sense of family commitment natural to most Italian families. The old and the young are treated with great reverence, caring and love. Life for this family is hard. A constant grind of days in the fields, of survival from season to season. There is not much time for sentiment but Julia's needs are met more than adequately and with great caring. I wonder about communication, even though she exhibits no outward signs of recognition or understanding, her constant smile and piercing bird-like eyes draw me in. I chat away to her and return her smiles, not knowing what reaches her soul. I am convinced that my small attempts at communication uplift her spirits.

After tea and a short chit-chat, Luigi and I pick our way back through the tunnel between the chicken poo and bowls and tin plates. We continue round the village and up the hill winding round the back of the church and up into the piazza in front of the church. This is the only point along the way that our house is visible. It peeks out from behind the trees, for a brief moment the red tiles brilliant among its close companions now roofed in modern dark slate-brown colored tiles.

Another example of how the various nuclei of villages and families have grown apart is the gossip among the oldies about the lovely daughter of one of the old inhabitants. She is a modern woman and her husband is a house-husband. She likes to work on construction or renovations and is remodeling her dad's old garage near the church, which now looks splendid in fresh white stucco with a new red tiled roof. But of course the consensus of opinion among gossipers from the other villages is that she should be home with the children and she should be cooking and cleaning for her man and she certainly should not dress in those appalling clothes. Those appalling clothes are short cut-off jeans revealing an expanse of muscled brown legs and an old t-shirt covered in paint. Topped off with a wild unruly mane of blond curly hair, she is a picture of delight and would fit nicely into any Canadian suburb. She is one of the few younger people here who can actually look you straight in the eye and have a good chat with lots of laughter. She is obviously a bit of a rebel, admitting that the more gossip she can generate the more rebellious she becomes. Anyway she is just a chip off the old block according to Luigi who says her father is just the same and relishes in causing dismay to the villagers by being different and not being part of the crowd.

Heading back through Giacopazzi, we can take the lower trail through some houses that rim a sloping piazza. This is where Paolino lives. He also likes to feed the cats and will buy good stuff for them from the butcher. There are at least eight cats here at various stages of life, sunning, playing or just sitting contemplating life in general.

The houses on two sides of the piazza are attached, some look very sad, vacant and crumbling, the families having left for something better never to return or the old folk have died off and the houses fallen into disrepair and decay. A whole way of life is slowly being lost. For those of us from the New World, it is obvious. Our history is minimal in comparison and it is incomprehensible that these little villages are left to die. My heart breaks a little when we go for drives around our valley in Canada and see the one hundred year old barns and miners cabins left to collapse and rot. So much history just ignored and lost forever.

The lane off the piazza near Paolino's house exits near my favorite house where the grandpa sits. We continue on our way home along the top road. Our chimney is smoking, the Aga is waiting, primed and ready to deliver. I wonder what Luigi will make for dinner? A veritable feast no doubt.

❖ ❖ ❖

Our usual evening routine was in full swing when a cousin from San Vincenzo, the Ferrari enclave, arrived informing us of a family reunion which was to take place on the coming Saturday. We had to go and she explained in depth how pleased and excited the clan would be to see their Canadian relatives. Reunion—quel horreur! To me this word conjures up a mass of people all stuck together in a hall, sitting at long plastic covered tables eating potluck if they are lucky, or mashed potatoes, peas, gravy and beef, numerous beers, lots of noise. Not my cup of tea! I have friends who groan as they read their invitations to family reunions. Every year they are dragged kicking and screaming by their own consciences to a remote Saskatchewan town or a downtown Dryden motel.

There are three things of which I knew nothing until I came to Canada, peanut butter, corn, and family reunions. Peanut butter came into my life when I was, unknowingly, pregnant with our daughter and I spent most evenings in front of the television with a jar of peanut butter clutched to my chest, attacking it avidly with a spoon. Corn was something we fed to the pigs in England. But up until now, the other thing, the reunion, I only had the shared agony of friends. My family is very small and very close in heart though not in distance, and a family reunion has never been a consideration. I believe English people to be quite insular and cool. The Anglo-Saxon veins are not filled with the hot, emotional blood of the Latins. Perhaps I only speak for my family but there were never family get-togethers, just the odd visit from aunties or grandparents, the occasional tea on grandpa's lawn.

After dragging up every excuse I could from my reservoir of unsociability, it was with immense trepidation and hesitation that I agreed to attend the great Ferrari reunion, Lorenzo's side of the family. The unmentionable side of the family who spawned this man who married Nona and then became a person tainted by Nona's hate when he left her and Luigi in New York. Uncomfortable in Costa Dazi and Rovinaglia, he returned to his village down the hill, San Vincenzo. Never again was his name mentioned in Nona's presence.

But here it was facing me, this dreaded reunion! I was fortunate indeed to have my art buddy visiting. One of her strengths was surviving reunions. She and Luigi wore me down and reluctantly I agreed to attend. The festivities were to take place in Bedonia, a nice town a half hour drive away up the Taro Valley from Borgotaro. I was stuffed into the back of the car with no hope of escape. The other two sat in the front chatting about how much fun it was going to be, wouldn't it be interesting to see how an Italian reunion works, do you think they tell jokes and get drunk and behave like idiots? Oh God, this was bad!

Clutching my friend's arm and drawing on her life-blood, we went to be swallowed by the throngs of Ferraris littering the steps of the Sanitario Della Madonna Di San Marco. Trying to find a bright side I considered that at least I would not have to spend hours participating in reminiscences because I could plead ignorance of the language. How silly, how naïve, representation from England, the United States, Australia was waiting just for me.

As the Monsignor was a member of the great Ferrari clan, we were allowed to use the special chapel for the family blessing, a beautiful church about which I gazed in wonder as the mass continued, revealing marvelous old oil paintings, gorgeous frescoes and the largest gathering of big noses I had ever observed in one location. It would not matter where I might be in the world I could pick a Ferrari out in any crowd.

Somewhere in the service the strains of a familiar psalm drifted into my consciousness and I was able to warble my heart out happily. It seemed like hours before we were released and even then I had to be introduced to Monsignor Luigi, all ninety-five years of him, and cousins Don Lino and Don Guiseppe Ferrari. Don Guiseppe had nodded off several times during the proceedings, amusingly so as he had to be nudged to perform his part of the blessing at the altar. It was quite apparent that he did not want to be here either as he left quite quickly after the mass for his camping and hiking weekend in the mountains.

Then came the family pictures on the steps of the church, which took at least an hour to organize. The frail old lady next to me was being supported by helping arms and told she could not sit down because they could not get her in the picture. I got my arm ready; it appeared she might die on the spot, but at least she would have her face in the picture. Then of course everybody had to take their own individual pictures.

As camera after camera was produced, things began to get out of hand. One authoritative gentleman stepped forward, bless his heart, and put a stop to it all by explaining that he would arrange for pictures to be sent to those who so requested.

We were then allowed some free time and leaving Luigi talking away somewhere in the middle of the huge gathering, I, and my friend, escaped into a haven of peace and beauty. We discovered a gallery of artwork donated to the Santuario from estates, from devout collectors, from philanthropists of beautiful, beautiful paintings, mostly religious in theme, some dating back to the Renaissance. We wandered the cool hallways and behind glass covers on the walls, we found the architect's detailed original diagrams of the construction and design of the dome and church and monastery, and we found the artist's plans for the frescoes, which had been completed in the mid-seventeen hundreds.

We were discovered hiding in the hallowed halls by a hurrying young lady, and called to lunch. Bearing in mind that Italian lunch is the main meal of the day I knew this would not be a hit and miss affair and prayed that there were no designated seating arrangements. That way I would squish between my two companions in a corner somewhere and remain unnoticed. In we went to a massive dining area, already packed to bursting. I was sentenced to a rollicking nasal Scotswoman on one side and two louder Londoners opposite. Conversation zigzagged across the table, from end to end, side to side, my ears rang, if I shut my eyes it all felt like noisy slicing lasers assaulting my brain.

And then came the food, platter after platter. Melanzzane, zucchini, those gorgeous little sizzled potatoes that I thought only Meri could prepare; porcini, chopped, sliced, baked, sautéed; veal parmigiano which I did not sample as I imagined all the poor little black and white calves being led to the slaughter. All this interspersed with sliced meats, proscuitto, mortadella, coppa, pancetta, wine, wine, cheeses, wine, wine,

bread, more wine, then desserts, trays of torta di mandorla
(almonds), fruit pies, little pastries, bowls of fresh fruit. Finally the coffee, I think I might have run away by now but I
smelled it coming and my heart began to sing. Perhaps I would
survive.

Some food was brought by guests, but most was prepared
by the nuns in the huge kitchen. The "head chef" was an
eighty-six year old nun, about four foot six, and as frail and
wizened looking as the end of a witch's besom, but that did
not fool anyone. The kitchen helpers knew who was in charge
and scurried round following her orders, she working almost
as hard as they. Students spending the summer studying,
sports groups attending soccer camps, all served the dinner.

Anxiously now, I began to devise ways in which I could
escape from the cacophony. The rollicking Scots woman, now
screeching in the thousand-decibel range, each Ferrari shouting louder than the next, I could hardly bare it any longer.
My brain was about to burst, my head was throbbing! Suddenly one of those magic moments occurred when a complete
silence fell. Oh good, it is all over, but no, now was the time
for entertainment. The lovely hurrying girl who had discovered us creeping through the hallways, produced a guitar
and all was restive and quiet as calmly and serenely her sweet
voice echoed through the hall with traditional folk songs. This,
however, was just a precursor of what was to come as request time began and thumping, bumping hands and feet
marked time with the good old Italian songs.

This Ferrari family reunion was apparently going to serve
two purposes, to renew old ties and discover new family
members, and also to bid Don Lino farewell and good luck
in his new position of Monsignor in Piacenza. The quiet,
unassuming, pale man with an insipid handshake, grew in
voice and stature as he stood on a chair and began to remi-
nisce, joke, sing, and laugh. He also informed us that we must
not miss his show in the planetarium on the top floor in the
dome. His life long love affair with the heavens had been

responsible for creating the only planetarium in the area. When he had finished his speech people stood to applause him. Perfect—my time to escape. I backed out of the door close by, followed by my friend, telling Luigi we were going to the planetarium. The peace and beauty of the dome was soothing and we sank into an oblivious rest as we awaited the rest of the audience and Don Lino. What a treat, we floated round the heavens in complete darkness beneath the midnight blue sky and sparkling stars and constellations. The only link to earth was the aroma of sweat and cologne and cigarette smoke.

All too soon it was over and with aching necks we exited after profuse thanks for the wonderful show. We found our way outside and wandered the beautiful gardens. Most people were somewhere else, still chattering I assumed, but we did encounter an American woman we had met at the dinner. Luigi and she had a more in-depth discussion about New York and laughing, she said, "We all have these people in New York, we just do not talk about them, but don't you get a zip out of knowing they are there?" Obviously a disguised reference to the Mafia, about which I knew nothing. Luigi replied, "Well not all of us!" She left smiling to herself in some sort of knowing way. I had heard about an old Uncle Frank in New York who may have had a slight claim to fame, if it was even true.

By now we had found our way into the parking lot, hot as Hades, we stood as good-byes, very emotional, very demonstrative, were prolonged beyond all belief. I have to admit it was a good experience enhanced by our discovery of the gallery and the journey through the universe. Apparently this reunion was a regular affair and I could anticipate attending each August. Perhaps next year we might arrange to spend the spring and early summer here and be back in Canada in August!

Ultimately, I was quite happy that my friend, now returned to Canada, had encouraged me to go to the reunion and by the same token it was only thanks to her that we "did Florence". She insisted that we pack up our backpacks and spend four days there. When we arrived at the Florence train station we went to the tourist office there (as prescribed in our tour guidebook, like good tourists) and entered the throng of backpackers waiting to find accommodation. When we finally had our turn it proved to be a good idea. Tell the staff how much you want to spend, which area you want to stay in, and they phone and do the rest.

We ended up after a fifteen minute walk, on the via Zanobi, at a private four or five story walk up, as befitting the area. When we gained admittance after talking to the lady in the speaker on the wall, we wondered what might become of us as we entered dark cavernous narrow hallways, thousands of round and round iron stairways! Would we be swallowed in the Renaissance and appear again as 15th century beggars or princesses? Finally on the fourth floor we were greeted with illumination and the lady of the house. She explained the light switch system of energy saving. Press the switch on the first floor and the light will come on giving one enough time to reach the room. Of course we could never get it right and just as we approached our door off went the lights making contact between the key and lock almost impossible. We found our very own "room with a view" through the lines of swaying laundry, across the wonderful red rooftops iced here and there with tantalizing falls of bougainvillea and geraniums. We could not see the Duomo but its close proximity became obvious a little later.

My energy was depleted and I collapsed on my lovely little bed and fell fast asleep while my friend went out to explore, loaded with three cameras and sketchbooks and bottles of water. It seemed only minutes later that an earthquake hit. The whole room shook as the offenders, all the bells in Florence, with the Duomo crashing like a huge gong, signaled some ungodly hour and I was shaken from my bed like a rag doll. By this time my friend had returned; we leaned out the window in awe of the bells and the setting sun.

But it was wonderful. How we enjoyed our stay. We walked and walked and entered every church and climbed to the top of Bruneleschi's dome, and marveled at frescoes, and stood in awe of David, and paid only for the Ufizzi. So much is free if you bypass the tours and special museums, although we did pay for and almost passed out at the beauty of the Chapel of the Medici princes in the Church of St. Lorenzo. The black marble floor set with other brilliant colors of marble in a wonderful mosaic. Marble adorned the walls and pillars, the sparkle and reflection was truly overwhelming. We spent hours in the huge market spending our last lire and then, totally overdosed on all the culture, we left that beautiful place and headed back to the peace and quiet of Rovinaglia.

❊ ❊ ❊

Luigi was always planning something. With four days of freedom from a wife who always knows best or at least will often say so, who knows what gargantuan changes may have been undertaken. Completing any work is an enormous challenge when the choice of tools is limited to the archaic array of grandfather's tools. Luigi had spent his "time off", gathering, cleaning ad displaying the old tools on the walls of the now sparkling clean cantina, as if in a museum. There were iron pointed shovels with a foot-pegs on the shafts designed specifically to smash your shin; wooden rakes with thick wooden pegs for teeth so heavy only Charles Atlas could drag them, a cast iron wheelbarrow with an iron rimmed wheel that jambs among the rocks and refuses to move like a stubborn donkey, cement trowels with broken points and wooden handles so old and split they come loose at just the wrong moment and hammers so heavy that if you could just hit the nail with the worn old head you would drive it home with one smash and numerous hand-held implements that might be more at home in the torture chambers beneath Bardi castle.

Luigi's four days of freedom had given us a greater appreciation of the history of the house and where it stood. The cantina was now more airy, opened up and lighter, at first I could not see how this could be, but the proud "curator" gave us the tour of his museum.

His most exciting moment had come when he demolished the bricked up piece of wall housing a door-shaped opening, built within the archway. It was now possible to see the whole length of the cantina with the end half framed in the gorgeous archway. He had discovered a deep rectangular rock-lined hole at the bottom of the archway on the east wall. As cleaning progressed he found a five-foot long chestnut board stretching across the floor beneath the archway, securely set between the flat rocks and earth. Thinking it might be a casket, he was wary to search further not wanting to disturb the remains; however, his curiosity got the better of him and carefully prying the chestnut up he discovered the hollowed out tree trunk. Further excavation revealed the trunk stretched across the floor from one end of the archway to the other. He was thrilled to learn from a passing hiker, also an historian, that this was a drainage system to allow ground water seeping down between the rocks in the hillside behind, to drain away into the fields. The system followed the Roman design and the historian, after examining the rock structure of the archway and the cantina, said that it was probably built about six hundred years ago.

The same wall in which the archway was set, reached up beyond the top of the cantina to form the end of our kitchen and sitting room, then on up into the loft, shaping into a central point. Luigi had been digging around in the loft, doing whatever it is curious Italian men do in lofts, when he discovered this was actually a double wall, confirming our idea that Nona's house was originally half its present size and butted up close to another house. In cleaning the rocks, some came loose and intending to secure them with cement, he removed them. Behind was the original end wall of the other house and built into what must have been a high small end window was an inscribed rock. The inscription was impossible to decipher but we were very excited about it. We intended to keep this little secret. Perhaps we would share it when we discovered the relevance, perhaps not.

With his bruised shins and knees, aching back and elbows, I wondered at the insanity of being too mean or stubborn to buy nice new, modern tools with which to accomplish the necessary jobs easily, almost pleasantly. The scythe, a monster thing with a long wooden shaft and halfway down a peg to grip, and a blade that would make the grim reaper look like a wuss, was responsible for the only space age entry in our ancient menagerie, a weed-eater. Having paid through the nose to have the old iron brute sharpened(not for the want of trying with grandfather's famous old whetstone) and almost slicing himself off at the knees, Luigi stomped away to the car and with gravel spitting from the screaming tires flew down to the hardware store, coming home with a weed-eater.

Unfortunately for the wild flowers and weeds the man with his new tool spelled doom. Everything growing fell prey to the blue plastic cord, spitting from beneath the roaring yellow machine. Wild roses, poppies, nettles, brambles, young sprouting oak seedlings, all was massacred as a swath was cut across the landscape. A little bunch of scarlet poppies, nodding their innocent heads from between the rocks of the piazza, were off limits though and continued to smile sweetly, defying death. My sister Jennifer's favorite flower, Luigi will not go near them having once felt the wrath of his very own wife as he and his machine came too close to these scarlet beauties. Others were not so lucky and fell prey to the hungry machine; however, I am quite convinced that the gods are on my side. Almost every time the weed-eater is prepped for its rampage, as it disappears down the hill with its owner to "tidy up", the clouds come rolling in, the rumbles start and the floodgates open.

Never one to waste a moment of peace, as the man and his machine disappeared down the hill, I set my yellow chair and drawing stuff out on the veranda and prepared my coffee, contemplating the merits of modern machinery. I was a strong hold out against the metal detector Luigi wanted to buy to hunt for the fabled gold cache left behind by the Germans after the war. If it had not been found by now, it never would. Besides with all the bullets which flew around this area, who knows how much live stuff might be lying in the underbrush just waiting to be detonated by a man with a metal detector. I had no sooner sat and sipped and thought, than the sun was obliterated as huge wafting indigo clouds rushed over the hills. I could still hear the weed-eater puffing and popping in the distance. The drops of rain began and I just managed to escape inside before the deluge. The time wore on, the rain continued. Eventually, when it weakened to light intermittent showers I set out on my rescue mission. Along the top road I met Paolino beneath a huge black umbrella. He asked where was my umbrella. I explained that I am a tough Canadian girl, that we do not use umbrellas, that I love a fresh shower. Five minutes later, with my tail between my legs, I rushed back to the house, soaked. Passing Paolino on his return journey was mortifying, I did not understand exactly what he said but obviously he thought it was very funny as he laughed his way on down the road.

Eventually a very wet, bedraggled, weed-eater operator arrived home, happy as a sandboy. Having cleared the footpath down to the piece of land called Banshoele he had sheltered in the old barn there, enjoyed his bread and cheese and occupied his thoughts with all sorts of ways to restore and utilize the barn. I did not tell him that I had plans for the numerous fallen, undamaged tiles. I thought I would save that for another time.

Beyond Banshoele there is a footpath that winds down through the woods along the perimeters of different fields and on down to San Vincenzo. In the past we have hiked the path through nettles so tall they can sting one's face, and brambles from which it is almost impossible to escape once snared by their thorny, grabbing tentacles. The intrepid mountain man would lead the way with Nona's old hand scythe and whack away at the undergrowth. I would bring up the rear very helpfully calling, "Mind that primrose; oh don't cut that lovely dog-rose;" how my head remains on my shoulders I do not know. Two hours later, stumbling out of the jungle we would arrive at the village just behind Uncle Angelo's house. Angelo is the only remaining brother of Lorenzo. The nicest, sweetest old man I have ever met, he is a joy to be with. I will collapse here on the old kitchen bench as the family, Uncle Angelo and his daughter Rita and son-in-law Angelo proceeds to chat away with Luigi, so happy to see us. When our daughter Melody ventured forth with her friend for their first international travel experience, they spent a few days with Angelo and Rita and her husband in their winter house in Parma and were treated royally. Even with her great love of Sicily, Melody still says Parma is her favorite city.

This trail has now become almost a simple stroll, thanks to the hungry yellow machine. We use the footpath frequently. A lovely walk through the old oak trees between the banks and hedges draped with wild roses, primroses and daisies. Given a new lease on life they peek out along the edges. I can now make the journey alone without fear of being swallowed by the Italian countryside never to be seen again. Luigi will meet me at Uncle Angelo's, and I can then be driven home up the tortuous road from San Vincenzo back to Rovinaglia. Of course one or two seasons of neglect and the trail will disappear, as nobody is interested in maintaining a footpath. There is more important work for the villagers, and I am sure each evening with breaking backs and aching shoulders, the old footpath would be the last thing on anyone's mind. With our imminent return to Canada, we did not again traverse the trail I now call "Primrose Lane".

Before we left, the usual sequence of shutting down No. 17 went smoothly and it seemed once again just a flash in time as we drove away down the road towards Borgotaro and our planned two-day trip to Munich. We intended to use the main route north as opposed to the autostradas so that we could enjoy northern Italy and the Tyrol. The weather was beautiful, we found a lovely little albergo in which to stay the night and Munich airport was as pleasant from which to depart as it had been for our arrival.

CHAPTER V

1999

We have spent both spring and summer seasons in Emilia. The autumn might be colder but we could harvest our walnuts and apples, and gather enough chestnuts to be ground into flour, all to be stored for the following year. We would also be able to cut our own firewood, enough for two years at least. Perhaps we are taking a lot for granted. Who knows how legalities regarding ownership of Nona's house will work out. My heart would break if I could not return to my beloved Emilian cottage.

This year will be a summer visit, my ill health the reason once again. A real winter of discontent as my bilirubins and white count misbehave and my body slumps to a very low, low. My heart and soul are strong. I know I will be well enough to travel in the summer, I just know this. We soldier on, my wonderful husband especially, running to the store to buy something to tweak my fancy, off and running again when whatever it was yesterday that was palatable tastes like poison today.

Anticipating legal fees, maintenance and utility bills for which we wanted to take responsibility (so sure were we that this year all would be finalized) we set up a bank account in Borgotaro from which Roberto could draw funds on our behalf and also, to ensure that Rosetta went to no expense of her own for keeping the house aired and clean. She is a darling and it was a long battle Luigi endured over the phone to persuade her to accept payment.

We booked the trip in anticipation of my recovery. I felt well by June and with medical permission granted, we sallied forth once again. The little house at the end of the rainbow waited. Continually planning this reno, that landscaping, we whiled away the flight to Europe fairly comfortably and Munich greeted us once again. After twenty or so hours of travelling and holdovers, we gratefully sank into the welcoming puffy duvets of Hotel Maria and slept like logs.

Driving all day was tiring but I did not want to linger. The draw, the anticipation of Rovinaglia was immense. And once again after the full day's drive, we pulled into the lane behind No. 17, safe, sound, and exhausted! Rosetta and her daughter Lorena had worked very hard. We unlocked the door and entered a little palace, sparkling clean with fresh flowers on the table. Two or three days recouping and we would be ready for action and adventures. Bedraggled as I felt I looked forward to Luigi's first discovery of a waiting castle.

He loves his newspapers, our siesta time will often see him outside on the sun chair beneath the shade of one of the walnut trees reading the local paper, "Gazetta Di Parma". It is a brilliant paper, the usual cross section of politics, highway slaughter, festivals, and Mafia reprisals seducing its readers into the pages. Most interesting to me are the weekly profiles of lesser-known historical sites. Castles, churches, palazzos, priceless artifacts and artwork hidden away from the general view but there to see if one knows where to look. Some of our most interesting adventures have had their origins in these informative newspaper articles.

We will set off in the morning and head down to the "Forno", the bakery where we choose our picnic for the day. My favorite, a local specialty is "Torta di Erba" a flat thin layer of crispy brown flaked pastry, covered with a mixture of leafy dark green vegetables, Parmesan cheese, egg, salt and olive oil. Throw in a couple of pieces of pizza, some real focaccia, and along with our apples and water, a fine feast fit for a king.

The simplest, most innocent discoveries are often the most memorable. One day, we set out for a 12th century castle and community out towards Piacenza, Castell' Arquato. The country roads led us through villages and farms, fields of alfalfa and wheat dotted with the ever-faithful scarlet poppies and blue corn flowers. Sometimes the poppies were so profuse they resembled scarlet carpets stretched over the hills between swaths of the early cut hay crops. Other fields of sage green, emerald, jade, lemon yellow, butter colored patchwork quilts of the most exquisite beauty, the squares joined together with seams of hedge rows, lines of Poplar, irrigation channels and the old dry rock walls. The views were too much, my eyes were not big enough. I needed more ocular capacity to take in all this wonder.

We often get lost when we are out looking for somewhere in particular, the roads crisscrossing and bending, unsigned junctions. We know in this particular instance we need to maintain a north-westerly course. The sun rises back there and sets over there. No problem, anyway, half the fun is trying to find these places. Eventually, we emerged from the maze and arrived about 11 o'clock in a small town we knew to be en route to Castell' Arquato. The church looked interesting and we needed some shade and a rest so we parked under some deliciously smelling trees hung with creamy white trumpet-shaped blossoms. Usually unlocked when in the center of the village, the churches offer a cool haven. We lingered inside, never tiring of the architecture, the historical significance of stone floors embedded with tomb stones, and steps worn by many feet, crucifixes, Virgin Marys, altars draped with intricate lace and red velvet, frescoes, domes, pillars and archways. Whether elaborate or plain, I always love the quietness and tranquility. I feel no guilt for being irreverent. I simply enjoy these churches for what they offer me. Museums, providing a look back in time.

Luigi, of course, found someone to talk to, the priest, so I went outside and walked around, hunting for any interesting inscriptions and dates. I rounded the corner of the campanile just as the bell started tolling its announcement of midday. Right above me, it was very loud, but not loud enough to drown out the call of a howling dog. She was behind a wire fence and stood like a wolf, nose to the sky, emitting a monotonous howl for the duration of the noise from the bell. Luigi then appeared at a doorway at the base of the bell tower and beckoned. I went in and there was the priest pulling the bell rope. Much to my surprise he offered me the rope. I was thrilled and fell right into the rhythmic pull. I could see the bell and wheel above me, and other bells hanging dormant. Childhood was far behind me but I had been a bell ringer for a number of years when I was twelve or thirteen. We had the youngest group of bell ringers, and George the Bell Master was very well known for producing well trained bell ringers. Trouble was that I loved to frighten my best friend outside in the dark churchyard and so she refused to go anymore. The dog was still there, although quiet now. The priest told us that she howls whenever the single bell tolls but never when they peal. He was so pleased we had stopped and very interested that I had been a bell ringer. He asked the name of the church and when I said St. Peter's he clasped his hands together in glee and said something about fate. This was also San Pietro, (St. Peter). I also thought it was amazing. The first time I had rung a church bell since I was a child and probably the last and we chose this place and precise moment in time.

"The occasion was certainly deserving of a good meal", suggested the priest, and recommended we go across the road and down to a pretty place with tables outside shaded with vines and umbrellas. He told us to be sure to tell them Don Reno had sent us. He waved goodbye and we had no choice but to go to that restaurant as he stood and watched until we sat down at a table. Oh well, the picnic would taste just as good for supper. Negotiating the usual deal, "just one plate of pasta each with mushrooms please, we do not want to pay more than ten thousand lire each", we sat at a table. The traditional manner of dining at noon is a three-course affair lasting at least two hours. The price can be hefty, even in the country. The workers stop their work for the afternoon, the farmers go back to their farmhouses, the shops close. This is the main meal of the day, usually eaten as three or four courses. There is no hurry, it is a time to relax and savor the food, enjoy good conversation. The "primo piato" will usually be a pasta, very often fresh and homemade, accompanied by mushrooms or perhaps a tomato and basil sauce. Parmesan cheese is plentiful and always sits on the table. The "secondo piato" will be a veal cutlet, some melanzzane or zucchini.

The "terzo piato" will be a fresh green salad of butter lettuce, perhaps some sliced tomatoes with fresh basil leaves. A supply of bread is unending and is eaten with everything. We cannot eat that much food at noon. Having lived in Canada for so long, feeding time is usually around six o'clock when the troughs open and we shovel down one plate filled with everything in fifteen minutes flat, forget the conversation, toss everything in the dishwasher and throw ourselves down in front of the television. The waiter says that there is no problem with us just having pasta. Of course it is homemade and delightful as usual.

When Luigi went in to pay, he chatted with the fellow behind the bar who amazingly enough had been a cook on a cruise line doing the Alaska run and was very familiar with the British Columbia coastal area. He had done a little travelling into the interior of the Province and knew about the Okanagan Valley where we lived. This was to be a day of coincidences indeed.

We continued on our way, but with stops to see this ruined church and that ruined castle, getting lost many times over, we gave up on Castell' Arquato this time and using the trusty sun as our marker headed back in the general direction of home. It was not unusual for our planned goals to disintegrate into a day of other discoveries. We would be able to do Castell' Arquato on another occasion.

❊ ❊ ❊

Always after a day's outing I am whacked so we usually use the next day to recover. I take lots of paperbacks to Italy and crossword books for my lazy times, and of course my drawing books. The library in Borgotaro is very nice but its selection of English language books is limited. Once in a while I will find a book of interest and as I had a fair number to donate I chose to go to town with Luigi instead of being lazy. Anyway it was Monday and I could not possibly miss Market day. What would all the old ladies say if I did not go. I really cannot explain the attraction, it is just something you have to do on Monday.

Wandering up one side of the market and down the other reveals nothing beyond the norm, but it is fun. Luigi had gone off for yet another meeting with the surveyor and now I wanted to sit and relax, and offload the usual market buys, bathroom mat, toilet brush, t-towels, and the usual kilo of parmesan which now weighs a ton, and of course more sunflowers.

I headed for another of my favorite bars on the corner of the piazza near the old prison and one of the larger churches in Borgotaro. It has the usual outside tables, flowerpots and umbrellas. I am attracted particularly to this one this year because the chairs are all now bright yellow, which I just love. I went in to get my coffee and stood waiting at the bar, considering that this time I might have to pay more if I am served at a table. The gorgeous young man behind the bar, however, insists, "Siedi, siedi, ti portero un café", so I went outside to sit and wait. I still only paid two thousand lire. He insisted on adjusting the umbrella for maximum shade and returned to his bar. I sipped my drug, and emitted a sigh of appreciation, no one can make cappuccino like an Italian. I pulled out my tattered sketchbook, no camera for me. I began to draw the old prison across the piazza, inhabited now only by the pigeons. I become lost in the architectural wonder of this 16th century building. Into the cracks and crevices I went with my pencil, feeling the dark depths beyond the iron-grilled windows. At home, in Canada, I will look back through my book and remember the sounds, the smells, the warmth, the breeze. I will remember every sensation of that moment in time, for years to come, while a flat piece of lifeless celluloid will lie, packed away in a box somewhere, long forgotten.

THE OLD PRISON   V. FERRARI

I was approached by a young woman and she asked if I am an artist. I told her I try to be. I sensed a commission coming, my worst nightmare. She asked if I do portraits, my explanation of how I work spontaneously for myself obviously lost to her. She rushed inside, dragging out the gorgeous young man from behind the bar. "Look," she said, "isn't he handsome?" Oh yes, he certainly was I thought, knowing now whom she expected my subject to be. "A surprise for his wife, my sister," she said. She was so exited, I found myself falling into the same old trap. I cannot say "no" and explained that I would do it another time. The now blushing young man was hauled away and his sister-in-law rushed off up the street in glee. How could she possibly understand that I need a face with character, one showing the ravages of time, a grizzled old woman or a face of great emotion, a woman wringing her hands in despair. My mood was completely broken, as I put away my drawing book.

Luigi arrived from his meeting with the surveyor who usually conducts his business, on market days at least, at a bar and restaurant near the town hall. He told me the bar is owned by yet another member of this ever-burgeoning family. The lady who owns this bar is also a Ferrari, a second cousin to Luigi. Her reputation far exceeds others in Borgotaro. When the Porcini Festival occurs, people come from far and wide to sample her wonderful secret recipe of pasta with mushrooms. Things must have gone well as Luigi happily related the details of the meeting explaining to me this document and that plan, a never-ending saga it seemed.

We began the lengthy, hot trek back to the car parked over the river in San Rocca. Parking in town is always impossible on Mondays. Whenever we cross the bridge, I wonder why it is necessary to have such a big bridge with six great arches striding across a few gravel bars, some dry mud and one or two stagnant puddles in which lazy fish circle. Only near the end of the bridge does anything like a river flow beneath us through the last arch. Familiar with Luigi's exaggerated childhood tales, I listened but hardly believed his description of torrents of water crashing down the river, when he was a boy. In Canada during the following winter a relative phoned to tell Luigi that the bridge was closed, water up to the railings, fields and farms upriver inundated and animals stranded. The water was sweeping through the old channels beneath the town and bubbling up through the drains to flood the poor old cobbled streets. After the devastating floods in November of 2000, I now have no doubt about the stories I was told.

When we arrived back at No.17, we found a plastic bag of fresh vegetables hanging on the doorknob. Marietta has been

down the hill again working in her garden, always a bountiful plethora of veggies. We love her. She is an absolute gem,
brown and wizened, thin white hair always escaping from a
natty bandana. Now there is a face to draw. She is bent double
with a poor old back and walks with an elbow crutch. A constant smile adorns her beautiful face, and she never fails to
offer a positive happy remark. I am never scared to ask her
how she is, for she is always well, regardless of how she really may feel. There are others, however, of whom you never
inquire as to their health, otherwise you will be trapped in a
lengthy description of every ailment possible, from poor knees
to aching backs to sore throats to varicose veins.

Marietta often hails us from amidst her spinach and onions and we wave back and shout our greetings, and when
on one day as she hailed and we waved, and she hailed and
we shouted, we thought nothing of it. Perhaps the wind was
obscuring our voices. We continued in this manner until the
wind bore her shouts of, "Aiuto," "help!" We quickly realized she was not simply greeting us after all. Rushing down
the hill we found her stuck between the old water barrel and
the fence. Having fallen she had no way of righting her
crooked old body. There she sat, laughing her head off at her
plight. Her crutch was stuck in the fence like a lethal weapon
and the old green hose-pipe whipped and writhed around
like a snake spitting venom. We could not help but laugh.
Between the two of us we managed to get her on her feet.
Luigi captured the green snake and she continued merrily to
work in her garden. Insisting that we avail ourselves of more
vegetables, I pulled one onion. "No, no, solo femmina", she
laughed.

"What is she saying?" I asked Luigi, wondering if I had
really heard her properly.

"You can only take female onions, not male", he said. I was
not aware there was a difference!

Once in a while I will join her and the other old ladies as
they while away the afternoons on her veranda, seated on

old wooden chairs, the stories and gossip in full throttle. The oft told tales of families, Sunday's mass, what happened at the market, who has done what, where and when. I will be drawn into the conversation and with my halting Italian, will stumble on. With the required hand waving and gesturing I manage to make myself understood.

One of the old ladies, a woman of whom you never inquire as to her health, is almost stone deaf. Often she will not wear her hearing aid. Her voice is raucous and ear splitting as she roars about in the conversation. Her husband is the sweetest, most gentle of men. He has the patience of Job, which he bloody well needs after sixty years of marriage to this woman. He smiles his way through her noise conceding to every interruption, knowing that she has not heard a word he has said. Bidding my farewells, amid much hand grasping and compliments about what a bella donna I am and how bravissima I am, I leave them to their repetitive, age old stories and return to the delicious smells of Luigi's cooking wafting out of the kitchen up the lane. I had a private giggle as I left this little gathering because for all of the deaf lady's bravado and control, I have seen her true colors. I was sitting on our piazza and without any intention of spying, now by which time I had grasped the fundamentals from the top road wanderers, I saw her stripped to her bloomers and bra sitting in the sun. I loved it. I love to see the real human side emerge from the stiff personalities.

Toiling away at the old wood stove, its top covered with pots and pans and the old kettle bubbling and splattering, the master chef was at work. Melanzzane, dipped in flour, egg and bread crumbs, sautéed to perfection and sprinkled with freshly grated Parmesan. Marietta's fresh green beans simmered lightly, whole and touched with just a little fresh, salt-free butter. Mushrooms chopped and sizzled quickly in very hot olive oil, with garlic and basilico and nice fresh unadorned mashed potatoes. With the required hunks of bread, bought fresh from the forno that morning, chunks of parmesan and wine in the middle of the table, we enjoyed our vegetarian fare. Being married to the best cook in the world far outweighs the disadvantages of being married to the only Italian in the world who can neither sing nor dance. Of course being from this part of the world he should be a good cook. Emilia Romagna is well known for its excellent cuisine, its famous arrays of prosicutto, mortadella, and bologna, the mushrooms and cheeses, pollenta, tomatoes and vegetables that are magically transformed into magnificent meals.

The usual dinnertime conversation occurred about tomorrow's plans. The original doorway in the kitchen had opened onto the little cobbled lane behind the house but was now blocked up. Above it, somewhere beneath the "lovely" new coat of grey stucco cement was the stone engraved with Luigi Dora's name and the year he built the house. We knew approximately where it was, having seen it the very first time we came with the children. Off we went to bed, having discussed this rock almost the whole evening.

The following morning I heard banging on the outside before I was even out of bed. I dragged myself into the kitchen, the church bell announcing the ungodly hour of seven o'clock. Long nails appeared at various sites through the kitchen wall. Finally, success! I heard a whoop and knew the great discovery was taking place. It took some careful work but eventually "Luigi Dora, 1883" was revealed. We were so excited but as usual the odd passerby up the lane could not understand our glee or why we had bothered. Uncovering this piece of history would be our last job this year, time to return to Canada was fast approaching.

We yearn each summer to spend more time in Emilia Romagna so we can do and see as much as possible while still having lots of time to be lazy. One of our children will always baby sit the house and cats and attempt at least to keep the flowers living in our parched, hot part of Canada. We eat here, we eat at home. We use gasoline here, we use it at home. Well, why don't we spend more time here? It is always my fault, as my son's t-shirt so aptly announced from his chest "Blame me why don't you—everyone else does." Not quite so, of course! The evil spirits always lurk, often choosing to reawake within and so back on chemo I go. Either I cannot travel because I can hardly function or I cannot be off the stuff for any appreciable amount of time. This year we had been fortunate enough to safely have a six-week hiatus. But how quickly it had passed. In no time at all it seemed, we were once again winterizing the house and closing it up which is a full day's work. We get started early.

In the past the mice and moths have had a hey-day, nesting and munching their way through cushions, linen, upholstery, and carpets. Every fabric and wooly yummy item has to be mothballed and packed in plastic. Silk flowers, baskets, all are fair game. Even the tires of Luigi's bike have to be hung beyond the reach of those hungry little devils. Mattresses must be protected against the rain. Our most insidious efforts to patch holes, and replace tiles will never be enough and it will always find its way in. Always, always, wherever we store the mattresses, drips will zero in on them.

Luigi takes care of the outside tasks, the cantina, the wood shed, draining all the plumbing, plugging water drainage outlets to prevent birds from nesting in them, and we tape sink and bath holes so that creepy things do not slither in. The picnic table is locked in the wood shed and the umbrella comes in to be mothballed. Finally the water and power are shut off. Last minute leftovers are given to Marietta and potted plants to Meri and of course fond farewells are exchanged, the villagers present in the farmyard to watch as we leave! As we close the door behind us once again, I cannot help feeling a little sad. This dear little house left unloved and lonely for another year.

After an arduous journey, we returned home to a sparkling house and verdant garden, fat lazy cats eyeball us from their sunny spots. "Oh, you're back", they say, "we managed quite well without you, thank you". I missed them like hell and this was their greeting. No rushing forward with tails held high, no hello Mommy.

Luigi spent months lighting up the fiber optic cables with trans-Atlantic calls, I wished we had shares in Telus. Will the legal rigmarole ever sort itself out? Towards the end of the year, I received the good news that, administered weekly for as long as it does the job, my new drug is transportable. My son "surfed the net" on his computer, a vile piece of technology that dominated the last ten years of my working life, however, I have to agree it was pivotal in helping me find the closest oncologist and hospital willing to take me on in Italy. Fortunately the hospital was in Parma, only an hour's drive from Rovinaglia. A placid, beautiful place, not too big, easy to navigate. We have enjoyed Parma's charm before, so rich in history, proceeding on her unobtrusive way through life. I dreaded having perhaps to go to Milan or another huge, mad, rushing, busy city, just the sort of place where I do not want to be.

Good things come to those who wait. We finally receive word after five long years, that the deeds to the house are ready and Luigi's signature is all that is required. No, the documents cannot be couriered to us. No, he cannot sign in the presence of a notary public, a lawyer, the Attorney General, the Governor General!

"Yes, Signor Ferrari, you must be here as soon as possible. The other members of the family are waiting just for you".

That stubborn brick-wall appeared from nowhere, "I have waited for five years, you can wait for me".

"When will that be, Signor Ferrari?"

"I am not sure, this month, next month, next year!"

We had waited for five years at the pleasure of lawyers, City Hall, provincial archives, Italian Consuls. There were phone calls, faxes of document after document, miles and miles of red tape. We had even awaited the healing of the Judge's broken leg, which had caused everything to come to a crashing halt. Delay after delay occurred as court dates were made and postponed. As often as Luigi asked, he was given the usual Italian run-around, lots of talk but no real explanation. The only person whom we honestly felt had bent over backwards and gone out of his way to aid us and try to get things on track was the surveyor. It was hard to be positive after the build up, the let downs, but we forged ahead with travel plans and hoped this trip would bring finalization to the legalities and we would be the true owners of the cottage, No. 17, Rovinaglia.

Chapter VI

2000

Spring brings a renewal of spirit and with it came Luigi's brightened feelings toward his Italian family. He felt he had kept them all waiting long enough. Our daughter, her dogs, her three-legged cat were happy to spend the summer here. One might easily believe the travel arrangements to be a breeze, considering this would be the fifth year in a row that we had made this journey.

After three months of searching for airline deals, convenient destinations, rental car, and just when everything was in order and departure dates were imminent, dear sweet Dr. Machiara, the oncologist in Parma, advised me to obtain my Italian passport, otherwise I may not receive free treatment in Italy. It was hard to get a straight answer, or the same answer from the Italian Consul. At first I was told I could not get a passport because I was not a citizen, then I was told I could because I had married Luigi while he still held Italian citizenship, and this I knew to be factual. Unable to establish from three different sources what paperwork I would need, I gathered together every piece of paper and document pertaining to my existence on this earth and headed off to Vancouver to apply for my passport regardless of whether I "may" or "may not" need it.

The first part was easy. My nephew who lives in Vancouver dropped me at the building housing the consul. Clutching my life to my chest, I rose slowly to the fourth floor. I found the office easily enough but getting in was another matter. The security was very tight. I almost expected to be patted down.

Eventually I had my turn at the bullet-proof glass with a tiny grilled hole through which I spoke. Between three different people and lots of misunderstanding, we finally agreed that I could apply for the passport, which I did. By this time it was noon and the office was due to close from noon to three o'clock. It is not hot here, why do they need a siesta? I completed the papers, I went away, I spent three hours roaming downtown Vancouver and sketching at English Bay. I withdrew the required amount of cash from the bank and tramped back, my poor feet throbbing. What luck, I was first in line and was received graciously. I think they saw the smoke coming out of my ears. I handed over a fifty-dollar bill and discovered they have no provision for making change at the Consul.

"But don't worry, we will reimburse you". "I don't care," I said, "I just want my passport." They assured me it would arrive promptly in the mail. "No, we will not use a courier," was the answer to my obvious question. I prayed that Canada Post would live up to its stated goals, and headed home. A week later, promptly as promised, my passport arrived. Taped, unbelievably, to the front was my six dollars and fourteen cents change. Oh the innocence of these lovely people, coming from a nation rife in corruption from the town hall to the highest levels of government, and no one will nick money from an envelope?

Five days later, we were on our way, anticipation and excitement completely blocking from our minds the ten hours stuck in a tin can, hurtling through the heavens at thirty five thousand feet. I compare it to having a baby. Five, ten, eighteen hours of agony, the brain is saying "Never again, never again", then the tiny wrinkled purple bundle arrives, ugly as sin, but to Mom, baby is the most beautiful thing in the world, and before long you want to do it all over again.

And so we land in Nice, after the usual cramped and tiring journey it seemed the most beautiful piece of tarmac in the world. Any piece of tarmac would have looked beautiful to us after that journey. Why Nice? Our weeks of research into the best car rental deals resulted in the fact that a Gold Visa or a Mastercard will allow insurance fees to be waived on the vehicle by the rental companies in France and Germany. Not in Italy, of course! Landing in Bologna, a stone's throw up the autostrada from Borgotaro, would be too easy. Adding the cost of insurance to the rental fee doubles the rental charges in Italy making them prohibitive.

Zooming off along the auto-route, I felt such a sense of coming home, knowing now that all that stood between me and that dear little house were four signatures and one hundred and four nightmarish highway tunnels most a kilometer or more in length. We crossed the now open border into Italy, with no more handsome guards wielding their Uzi's to confront us. The European common market has taken care of that.

Luigi's theory is "go with the flow". With the flow doing 140 km per hour and certainly not the required number of car lengths between us all, we flew along the coast and through the tunnels. Glimpses of the sparkling Mediterranean, hilltop towns and spewing industrial chimneys flashed between tunnels along the Autostrade Del Fiore, the Highway of Flowers, but these punctuations did nothing to allay my gut wrenching, white-knuckle fear of driving, or should I say being driven on these highways of madness. I wondered if saving the cost of insurance fees was worth our lives. I consider these highways of death to be a form of population control. Forget about wheelchairs and walking sticks. Just bring on the pine boxes and stuff the leftovers in. The death rate on the autostrada in particular, is astonishing. Perhaps it is hard not to emulate the scarlet Formula One Gods, Schumacher, and Barichello. After all the country almost declares a national holiday when a Ferrari wins a Grand Prix. After five hours existing a hair's breadth from death, it is a journey I do not care to repeat. We arrived in Rovinaglia, exhausted, organs and brains still hurtling along in stationary bodies.

Our exhaustion, however, did not extinguish our feelings of happiness and satisfaction knowing that the house would soon be ours. We surveyed our domain of overgrown jungle. Grass and weeds had devoured the piazza and knee high ground elder choked the rose garden. The pathway to the wood shed and round the house was lost beneath a blanket of last year's dense, matted brown grass. The wild flowers I collected and planted last year were indistinguishable amid a veritable field of dead straw colored hay. Even Meri's good old chickens had deserted this impenetrable mass. The anticipation of what we knew it could look like, spurred us on.

We have had our own key for a couple of years and no longer have to claw our way into Meri's pitch black barn, fighting through the spiders' webs for the nail on the back of the door where the key used to hang. I opened the door, stepping over the delightful carpet of leaves and debris blown under the door and spread across the kitchen floor during the winter. It did not matter, they were our leaves on our floor. Looking at Luigi, I saw so much emotion. I knew he was thinking about his Mom and all the years of hardship she endured here. But she was happy then and I knew she would be pleased to see her little house loved once again.

Opening up the house after our long absence is always exciting. As tiresome as it may seem I get great satisfaction from hanging all the smelly mothballed blankets and quilts out of the windows. Going outside and looking up at the bedclothes, their hibernation over, swaying in the breeze, their colorful lives erupting from the windows, I felt I had the knack. My windows now looked like every other country window when everything is flung out to air each morning. My diligence at mothballing paid off. I had managed to keep the mice and moths at bay this time. However, spiders' condominiums festooned every corner, the beams, even the naked light bulbs hanging on old wrinkled wires had lovingly placed webby shades. The resident lizards were not bothered by my presence and danced their ways up the walls to the windows where they paused on the bed linen, part of the family. They would be back tomorrow sunning on the window ledges. A single shiny black scorpion had managed to find its way through Luigi's duct taped plug hole in the bathtub, a cute little thing about an inch long, tail raised, ready to do battle. I scooped it out and sent it on its way. Would it ever appreciate its good fortune in not being discovered by Meri. It dashed away down through the floorboards, off and down into the cantina to see what Luigi was doing!

After a monumental effort the adrenaline was waning. Sitting at the still dusty table I had a quick sip of my favorite wine, Lambrusco, a nice light mid-sweet wine with a sparkly tang. Giulio would not approve, "That is not wine," he would say. The wine he drinks is like caustic vinegar, home made and dry, so dry. But I do not care, I have never been a connoisseur, I just drink it because it is cheap and it tastes good. I remember bringing a bottle of Canadian wine for Giulio on an earlier visit. Luigi explained the significance of the Okanagan Valley, how our wines had won worldwide acclaim and medals. He chortled in his cheery way and said it was not wine, it was water, and of course the best wine in the world was "grown" in northern Italy.

Luigi had not informed the family of our intended arrival time, intent on causing no disruption in their lives. He does, however, have the ability to smile sweetly as he nettles his way under my skin. I suspected he was doing the same to Meri but I kept my silence. I wonder if it is his personal defense against the Iron Lady. We had arrived as quietly as possible planning to get everything up and running and get our second breaths. I knew he anticipated even more haggling despite the fact the battles of the last five years should be coming to an end.

How naïve, did we really believe we could sneak in, sight unseen? Tap, tap at the door, "Avante", I shouted, unable to heave my exhausted self from the chair. In came Meri, carrying a basket laden with fresh vegetables, eggs and a bottle of Giulio's delightful wine. Doing the hugging and kissing thing we conversed with the usual animation. Meri is always so concerned about me and my health. When Luigi came in, she immediately launched into a streaming tirade. Why did he not tell her when he was coming? So many things have to be arranged, lawyers, surveyors, they have all been kept waiting, the taxman, the electricity man, and the bank? I can never understand the obsequious nature of these village people, having spent so many years in Canada where we are all considered equal regardless of our health, our employment or unemployment, where one neighbor is a doctor, another a logger, and all the kids play street hockey together. Luigi is not sucked into the whirling vortex and finally, out of breath she leaves, perhaps believing she is still the reigning matriarch, even over her little brother. I leaned out of the window to breath deeply and calm down and I was greeted by Nona's special climbing rose that I pampered and cosseted last year, willing it to take on new life. It had shot up the wall, under, over, through the iron railing of the porch and was nodding little pink faces at me from just beneath the window ledge.

About to withdraw into the house I heard a young voice calling up to me, "Zia Ginnie, Zia Ginnie", looking down I saw Gloria. Having blossomed over the past year, Gloria, now fourteen is almost my height. We have had a special bond with her and her family. The little family that lived in Lorenzo's house in San Vincenzo, who have worked so hard to make it into a beautiful house, have always shown such caring and interest in their Canadian relatives. For five years I have corresponded with Gloria, struggling valiantly with her English, she has endeavored to overcome the communications barrier. She has been responsible in part for my advancement in her language, sending lists of useful words, conjugating verbs, drawing pictures and labeling them in English. Of course she is simply an extension of her own family, her inner and outer beauty coming from her lovely mother, and her dad, Stefano, Meri's second son, so different from his siblings, his mother. Calm and easy-going, with a sense of humor like his Dad, he never complains about any hardships that descend upon him. They live away from the petty whining life of Rovinaglia in the village of San Vincenzo down the hill via Primrose Lane or a short drive down the tortuous gravel road. I am convinced all the happy people live in San Vincenzo, and all the miserable people shouldering the worries of the world live in Rovinaglia.

When I think back to the time we visited all those years ago, I remember Luigi trying to keep secret our visit to San Vincenzo, to the cemetery where his father is buried. Nona was a strong willed, powerful woman. She never forgave her husband for returning alone to Italy from New York to live out his life in his little cottage. He deserted her and their son. Knowing Nona as I did, having spent the first couple of years of my marriage to Luigi living with her in England, it was easy to believe that she might have been a very difficult woman with whom to live. There would not have been much peace and harmony in their home. I learned early on that she was a strong, dominating woman. There was never a mention of Luigi's father, even at get-togethers with his other sister and her family living at that time in England. San Vincenzo did not exist, except perhaps in hell, the feud perpetuated by a few of the old diehards continues.

Gloria was thrilled at our arrival and soon rushed away to tell her Mom we were here. It was not long before the rest of her family arrived and our little kitchen was bubbling with chattering people. They never overstay their welcome and left after securing promises from us that we would go down to their house for supper on Sunday.

The more often we visit Rovinaglia, the easier it becomes to settle back into the routine of village life, a way of life and culture so different from our own and yet we slip in like hands into familiar old leather gloves. At first, what seemed inconvenient hardships, have now become experiences of relative enjoyment. Our survival here comes from lessons learned in acceptance, tolerance, and a huge great bucket of patience.

Several frustrating trips downtown in the afternoons to pick up an essential item, without which we cannot possibly live, only to find the town closed for siesta, ensure I no longer forget. I have learned the fine art of simply doing without. Having the capacity to think ahead can be very useful. I have never been the kind of neighbor who drops by to borrow a cup of sugar or a litre of milk, however, I will nip down to Meri's and get some eggs or half a loaf of bread. And Marietta and the "Deaf Lady" are always begging me to raid their vegetable gardens.

I have also learned to get the box of sticks and firewood in the night before. Fighting my way through the wind and rain to the woodshed at seven o'clock in the morning can be gruesome when the previous evening's gorgeous sunset had assured me of "shepherds' delight".

If it is Thursday and the shops are closed all afternoon and evening, which is a common European practice and there is absolutely nothing in the fridge, either we grub for roots and berries or go for a pizza. And if we are starving at five o'clock, well too bad, because nowhere opens for supper until seven o'clock, and then it is at least a forty-five minute wait.

If we are lucky we might notice the two lines on the back page of the newspaper which tell us there will be a gasoline strike the next day. Empty tank? Stay home, even if it is a chemo day. Rail strikes are common and sometimes unannounced so if we had planned to go to Cinque Terre tomorrow we should phone Roberto, who works for the state railroad, to confirm the trains are running, otherwise we may have dragged ourselves down to the station at five o'clock in the morning for nothing!

Even the polizia work on a hit and miss basis. You will see them leaning up against their cars, in their immaculate uniforms and jack boots, so good looking, smoking their cigarettes, eyeing the beautiful women. One day fly by at ninety, they will ignore you, another, mosey along minding your own business, they will pull you over. We were pulled over one day, the polizia demanded every piece of paperwork on the car and Luigi's license, which he would not accept as valid. The officer said it looked like a fishing license. We have been told so often that Canadians do not need international licenses but this policeman was adamant. We had twenty-four hours to present the license and the original copy of the car lease, which is always left at the rental office. We never did show up and the next time we were pulled over the same policeman appeared to have a lapse in memory and was quite satisfied to chat and walk round the car. Oh, what a country! I love it!

During the past few years, our evenings in Rovinaglia had settled into a comfy routine. No television, no radio, no telephone to pollute our senses. Just peace and tranquility! Luigi would often head off to gossip in the garage with Giulio, or walk round the village, chatting with anyone, everyone. Italians love to talk. I, with my coffee, feet up, reading, drawing, doing crosswords, doodling little plans and room configurations of how we could move stuff around to make more space for convenience, for aesthetics. The end of another day, what will we be doing tomorrow I thought as I confidently scribbled out room changes and floor plans. We needed some groceries, thank goodness it is not Thursday, and I have to get some white paint to do the bedroom window. Off I went to bed, dead asleep by the time Luigi came home from his rounds.

Leaving my ideas on the table was a mistake, now that Luigi felt free to make changes inside the house. "Leonardo" was up at the crack of dawn, revising, inventing, and implementing. I always consider each day to be an adventure filled with discovery, invention, frustration, satisfaction and even humor and this was to be no exception. Having concussed ourselves so often on the top support beam of the midget door way between the kitchen and dining room, I had designed a plan for filling it in with bricks and opening up the main wall, allowing free flowing access between the kitchen and dining room. A more open plan would also allow more light and enable heat from the kitchen and the wood-stove to circulate on cold days. The kitchen often became an oven itself as the heat from the wood-stove had no escape. An impatient man, when he has a plan afoot, Luigi was heaving the sledge hammer at the wall, before I had time to move things out of the way or protect the rest of the house from dust. I made pathetically valiant attempts, hanging sheets of plastic, putting away as much as I could into cupboards. This dividing wall having been constructed in more recent times of brittle, hollow red bricks, came down in a flash. Shards of brick flew everywhere, lethal weapons embedding themselves in the other walls, in my lovely old table that we had only bought last year. I had not thought about moving one of my watercolors of a sunflower and the poor thing was stabbed through the heart. Fortunately I had never had a piece of glass cut for the painting.

I did not know that one twelve by six foot wall could produce such a massive pile of rubble and began shoveling it into buckets for Luigi to carry out. A right brainer from day one, a more logical method of removal did not occur to me. Luigi took command and within the hour the whole lot had gone straight out the window. As I worried about Marietta or Lena being buried in rubble, he assured me he had roped off the footpath with warnings of danger.

The dust was incredible. It coated every surface in the house; the walls, the windows, the toilet seat, the bathtub, the bed covers, the onions and garlic. It had puffed its way into drawers and cupboards, into cups and pots and even down the spout of the teapot. I now saw how pathetic my attempts at dust proofing had been. I did, however, have the foresight to wear a mask and felt somewhat vindicated as Luigi sneezed and coughed his way through the mess that was left from his demolition of the wall between the kitchen and dining room. The only problem was that now no available wall space remained for Nona's huge sideboard. Sorry Nona, but it was the most hideous piece of furniture I had ever laid eyes on. It did not take "Leonardo" long to invent a better way to utilize this monster. Chopped, sawed, and nailed, two separate units were born out of this great behemoth. The rest went out the window! Now functional and later beautified with a few coats of paint, we were able to place them in vacant and newly created corners.

We had managed with the three-burner gas stove stuck beside the bathroom door for four years. To create working surfaces of which there were none except for the fold down top cover of the gas stove, an executive decision was made to line up the washing machine, the gas stove and the wood stove along the wall beside the midget sink. A great idea sir, but as always one thing leads to another.

"As we are moving everything around, why don't we just slide the wood stove a bit to the right and we can fit in a new sink?" said he.

"Have you measured?" said I.

"Of course," said he, showing me his three-finger, four-finger infallible measuring method.

During dinner we decided that tomorrow we would drive the hour to Casa Mercato, the only department store in the vicinity where we could buy anything from a safety pin to a kitchen sink. Perfect!

We did not rush off too early as we had things to do in town. Arriving at Casa Mercato to closed doors was to be expected. Once again we had failed miserably in the "think ahead" department, it was siesta time and everything had come to a standstill. A bit peeved, but prepared to wait, we drove off to explore.

Everything happens for a reason. The delay resulted in us making a wonderful discovery. Just past Alseno, a little town on the Piacenza plains, and out along a country road, we found a 12th century monastery. The red brick construction was quite different from our area, and I was, as usual eager to sketch. There wasn't a soul around and I felt a little guilty peeking through cracks in the church doors, and trying to see through the grills. Luigi forged ahead, found an open door and was welcomed by one of the Brothers of the "Frati Di Chiesa San Bernardo Il Fondatorre", arms tucked in sleeves, his robe tied loosely at the waist with a cord. He floated quietly ahead leading us round the arcaded court-yard and through the cloisters. He pointed the way through an archway where we entered the church and walked silently round this cool dark place marveling at the construction, the pillars, the worn stone floors, stepping over old Latin in-scribed marble slabs protecting the bones of long ago men of faith. I resolved, as I do every year, to get a book of Latin translation. I could now decipher dates but the inscriptions were always a frustrating muddle.

We were most intrigued to discover an open area in the floor at the base of a column. Looking down and inside the excavation was amazing. Touching a rock floor at least two feet lower and feeling around the hidden base of the pillar below the current floor of brickwork, it was evident that the building existing here now had been constructed on the site of a church built much earlier than this one. Restoration was taking place in other parts of the monastery and in talking to a worker, Luigi discovered that this man's life was his bricks. He was a mine of historical information. I was surprised to hear how brick construction had been a sign of great wealth and status, whereas the poorer members of society used rock to construct their homes.

I wondered if the remains of the church beneath this one had been a reflection of the true poverty and self-denial of its residents and the surrounding community. Did this 12th cen-tury brick architectural beauty tell us something different about those who went before?

We came crashing back into the present as the bells clanged above indicating three o'clock. Heading back into the 20th century we ventured off to find our sink.

I prefer and need to keep my stress level almost at flat-line. And so, having walked round and round the most square feet of any store on the planet, watching Luigi do his four-finger thing on every sink in the place and listening to him discuss the merits of this double-sinked stainless steel one, that single-sinked porcelain one, draining board this side, that side, guarantees, prices, my assertion tremored and bubbled and rose to the surface like Vesuvius. Within five minutes I had measured, selected and announced that we would take this one and I added two new cabinets to hang on the kitchen wall. Nasty, nasty, but necessary! We soothed each other's troubled hearts by treating ourselves to a quasi Persian tapeti, a nine by twelve rug for the draughty old wooden floor in our new open dining-cum-sitting room.

Arriving at the pick-up area, we opened the hatchback. Out of the warehouse came three huge boxes, one containing the sink/draining board unit, the others the cupboard units, followed by the biggest nine by twelve rolled carpet I had ever seen. The following circus of events reminded me of record breaking attempts at how many people can fit into a volkswagon. Puffing, panting, sweating, putting in this way, that way, taking out, rearranging, stuffing in again. It was very amusing, at least from my perspective, seated in the shade on a typical humid, hot Parma day. Told by anyone, even an expert, that something is impossible gives Luigi all the more reason to prove them wrong.

That tiny, trusty all-purpose Fiat did not let him down. With string and rope and red plastic waving, the hatchback forced down upon the sticking-out boxes, hinges straining, and with the massive rolled carpet jammed in between our heads like a cannon ready to fire straight through the windscreen, we departed amid cheers and roars of laughter, arms raised to the sky, and one man making the sign of the cross, knowing that once again we had left behind an impression of complete insanity, "Mama mia, quell Canadese matte!" Obviously the same employees from the previous year when we completed the same operation with a fridge, and the year before that when we must have set a Guinness world record fitting two huge armchairs into a two-door hatchback. Those men knew we were crazy Canucks and accepted our stuffing techniques without question.

I am sure we broke every known transportation law as we snuck home via country roads hoping not to encounter any over zealous polizia. After two hours trapped inside the car, knees jammed up against the dash board, and Luigi with elbows squeezed to his sides, wrestling with the pedals and gear shift, we arrived safely home. Unfolding our bodies from the tiny tin box, we dismantled the Chinese puzzle, hauling and dragging it all along the lane, down the cobbled uneven path to the house, up the steps and into the kitchen. An exercise in sheer determination, in sweat, and much giggling on my part which produced flame from Luigi's nostrils.

Chucking our fanny packs, leftover rolls and cheese, and bottles of water on the table, we sank with sighs into our beautiful Ferrari red easy chairs (from another stuffing expedition), threw our legs on the footstools and tossed down the required amounts of Lambrusco and Merlot. We talked about the day's events and tomorrow's plan of action. I finally got the old man laughing and off we went to Eliza's for pizza, to sit in her beautiful restaurant surrounded by flowers and to look out over the stupendous view to the northwest, the sky ablaze with a gorgeous sunset scalding the rooftops and hillsides.

The next morning, I could not wait to roll out my carpet. Having felt very guilty about the sink episode, I had let Luigi choose the color and design. Big mistake! Rolling it out, I was pleased with his choice of colors, a mixture of reds, blues, yellows and greens on a wine red background. Perfect! It picked up some of "my yellow phase" and other colors in cushions and paintings. It would hide the dirt so no need to buy a vacuum cleaner, I could continue to swish my way around the house with my birch twig bezum. Nice pile too, I thought and looked down at my toes nestling nicely into its coziness. And then I noticed the design. What had been a mish mash of pretty colors glared up at me in all its awfulness! Medieval hunters on rearing steeds, spearing and stabbing beautiful deer, dogs ripping out their throats, falcons with talons outstretched, descending on poor innocent little birds. This massacre was contrary to my beliefs. Unable to squash an ant, a spider, unable to eat anything which has a brain, a heart, blood, feelings, vehemently opposed to hunting and the killing of animals for food, I stared aghast at the slaughter beneath my feet. However, counting to ten and doing my Zen, I decided this would be one time I would keep my mouth shut and my thoughts to myself.

Back in Canada we had talked as usual, about how we could improve Nona's house, but I was adamant that we should not undertake any hard, backbreaking work. For the last couple of years I was only the cleaner-upper, watching Luigi filling the gaping chasm of the old derelict house, and raking and shoveling and leveling for grass, many times over moving rocks and paving stones from here to there, building the arbor, performing never-ending, toiling, sweating jobs. I did not want us to wear ourselves out again. Pushing the broom and mopping the floor was the limit of my duration.

How soon we forget, inserting enticing little suggestions in his dinnertime conversation, "Wouldn't it be nice if…," or, "I love those re-pointed walls at Paulino's place." "Why don't we…?" and so on.

"Yes, yes, yes," I agreed, but Oh God—the work involved. "We should ask your nephew Roberto to do it," I say.

"No, I want to do it myself."

"Well, how about asking the "Tractor Boy" to help you."

"I want to do it myself," he repeated firmly.

I admitted defeat only a week after we arrived. Having jet lagged like crazy, I could not even mop the floor but now sweeping up Luigi's mess does not seem so tiring.

I have learned over the years that my husband is a "one-thing-leads-to-another" worker. I cannot count the number of times he has intended to fix something, a dripping tap, the dryer, a leaky dishwasher, always starting out with the best will in the world. Four and five hours later, he is cursing and moaning as he disappears into the nether regions of the basement to mop up the pond that has gathered from the pipes that come down from the kitchen that join to the U bend that goes up through the counter to the tap where the washer was being replaced! "Oh it will only take me half an hour," he says. "Oh yes, I have heard that before," I say, at which time he stomps off all defensive. I cannot stifle my wicked English sense of humor.

And so this little innocent Italian house presents the same challenges. Today we will remove the ancient glass fronted windows and shelves from Nona's old china cabinet set into the rock wall. Easy peasy, a hammer, a screwdriver, a chisel, and some muscle. Not so, the hinges of the windows are attached with rusty nails as long as screwdrivers. The nails are sunk deep into a solid, old chestnut framework. Oh well, the whole lot is coming out anyway so we will just use the sledgehammer and a crowbar and be done with it. I saw the potential for these lovely old windows and did not help the situation by insisting that they be removed without damage. That finally achieved, the beautiful hinges mangled and bent beyond repair, we carry them safely outside.

The two-inch thick chestnut shelves are firmly embedded between the rocks. The sledgehammer begins to fly and I know now that it is time for me to leave, as pieces of rock and splinters of wood begin to fly through the air. Clean up will be fun!

Three hours later a triumphant man appears, covered in dust and sweat. "Come and see, I have a great idea," he says. The now naked hole in the wall measures about three feet by six feet and is about two feet deep. The "great idea" is to fill in from the floor up to about three feet with rocks, and insert flat rocks here and there above that up to the beam, like small shelves and put wine bottles on them. The idea did not seem great to me. We had originally discussed a completely differ- ent plan. To repair the inner rock area to give it a uniform look (crooked and un-level things have no place in my life) and after filling the bottom half of the opening with rock work to resemble the current wall, top it off with a nice long flat rock to make one decent inset shelf. I had intended to place the bottom half of the old credenza in front and thus create a nice area behind it to put the baskets of onions and garlic and also the wine bottles. We never agree on anything anyway so this was no different. I cleaned up all the mess and then off I went outside trying to pretend to myself that Luigi's idea would work out well and look nice. My ham- mock rocked me into a more understanding mode. "Let him do what he wants," I said to myself, after all did it really matter?

Much hauling of rock and mixing of cement took place, buckets of water, and hose pipes through the window, crash- ing and banging and some sort of Italian laced with Canadian expletives.

Called in once again, another three hours later, I vowed to say it looked great. It did not. It looked awful. This was not a grotto in Amalfi, this was supposed to be my nice Italian hill- top house rock kitchen. I did, however, say that it was very nice, but made the fateful mistake of saying that the long flat rock along the bottom was crooked. I escaped quickly to the serenity of my cover under the walnut trees and swung again in my hammock, starving, but daring not to enter what now sounded like World War III. I went down to Meri's kitchen and stole a piece of hazelnut pie from the table.

What began at eight in the morning as a "simple job" ended at seven o'clock. A gargantuan effort of strength, toil, and sweat presented itself to me. The opening was now completely filled from top to bottom. I had my flat rock kitchen wall alright, but no shelf, nowhere to put wine bottles, onions or garlic baskets. The new rockwork was still a bit crooked but

I certainly was not prepared to put my life on the line by being critical. We each then reversed our position. I saying that his original design looked lovely, he saying it had looked awful and finishing the wall properly looked much nicer. A truce of sorts!

Luigi disappeared into the shower and I began again the massive cleanup of centuries old dust, plaster, clay, rock and gobs of 20th century cement. Eliza's pizza sounded good. Arriving at nine o'clock, we collapsed into two hours of heaven, of pizza, wine and cappuccino, and even a few tired laughs.

Hanging the kitchen cupboards was the plan for the next day and we rose early ready to tackle the job. Trying to drill holes in solid rock is not easy, especially with Meri hovering with her comments about more paperwork and her paranoia about "important people" at its peak! The screws for the brackets had to be cemented into the wall for stability. Spirit levels, like tape measures have no place in Luigi's life. He eyeballed the brackets and was not happy after hanging the cupboards, to see that one was crooked and one was lower than the other. By guess and by golly does not always work but far be it from me to introduce any helpful ideas into the situation. The knowledge gained during my eighteen year "apprenticeship" with my father as plumber's helper, carpenter's aid, electrician's assistant, among other things, was best not mentioned at this particular time. Much ranting and raving was occurring and stirring the raging waters would be unwise. I dutifully carried tools, held up corners of cupboards and swept and stood to attention. The usual "two hour" job had become a marathon.

At two o'clock I downed brooms and, negotiating my way across a floor littered with an array of tools, the ages of which spanned a least a hundred years, I gathered together nutrients for the starving worker. Forcibly removing the wrench from Luigi's hand while on his knees under the old sink, I pushed him out of the kitchen door to the picnic table. Once seated and with food in his stomach he conceded he was tired and that it might be best to quit for today. "We can always straighten the cupboard tomorrow," I said, which was daring of me, but necessary. And perhaps cruel, as I could see he was so tired, if the cupboards had fallen off the walls at this point they would have stayed where they lay. Thank goodness tomorrow was Wednesday, the cupboards would have to wait. My first appointment at the hospital loomed. At least we would have a day off from the coal mines.

❊ ❊ ❊

We left at nine o'clock, equipped with everything I could possibly require, syringes, porta-cath needles, intravenous lines, connections, saline, drugs on ice, all carried from Canada. I have never been in doubt about my condition or my health care. I have those strong Anglo-Saxon shoulders that can hold up the world. This day, however, the nearer we got to Parma, the more apprehensive I became. As we found our way to the hospital, the street names in the vicinity amused me, via E-Coli, via Sanguinetti (thin blood), and via Cadavero (which I thought was "cadaver"). We could not help but chuckle and my spirits began to rise.

Finding, eventually, a shady little spot on E. Coli in which to park, we walked to the hospital, heading for Oncology and my ten o'clock appointment. Running the gauntlet across the hospital grounds was akin to Russian roulette. Cyclists were everywhere, crossing and re-crossing like the Royal Canadian Mounted Police musical ride. Green coated and hatted men, stethoscopes flying, white-coated, purple-clogged nurses, coats streaming out behind like Bat-Man, all sorts of hospital employees with bicycle baskets full of files, we eventually placed our complete trust in them and just strode across the grounds. Proving their innate ability to avoid anyone or anything, they crisscrossed each other and flew between parked cars, ambulances, pedestrians, any obstruction in their way.

Opening the door to the waiting area and reception, my

chin must visibly have dropped in amazement at the sight before me. At least one hundred people were sitting, standing, waiting. Numerous bald heads, yellow, pallid faces, surrounded by support groups, husbands, fathers, wives, mothers, aunties, grannies, great-this's-and-that's and others, all set in somewhat archaic, dull surroundings. Floating among this misery were the ever-present Italian beauties, women in flowing dresses, gorgeous wigs rich red and henna and golden tresses, gold dripping from wrists and necks and ears, gorgeous soft leather sandals. So uplifting to my soul, at least. Hard plastic chairs were arranged in boring rows, dusty fake plants and one co-ed washroom for visitors and patients alike, a cardboard sign hanging on the doorknob announcing "Aperto" or "Occupato", the user having to switch the sign on entry and exit. One sink with a dripping cold water tap, no soap, and some long paper towels that came out four or five feet at a time when pulled. Where is my beautiful Oncology? Its twelve lazy-boy style, soft seated chairs in a waiting room of restful taupe, sage green and dark rose décor, the tropical fish tank brimming with color and life?

Checking in amid the confusion of whom I really was, was very funny. My Canadian passport announced Virginia Gabriella Ferrari; my Italian passport announced Virginia Gabriella Colbourne. Very often Italian females retain their maiden names after marriage.

"Who exactly am I?" I asked Luigi.

"Don't ask me," he said, I have been married to you for thirty-four years and even I do not know that."

I would be Gabriella Colbourne for the duration. Perhaps Gabriella sounded more familiar to them. At least we had a laugh as we squeezed in among the throngs, amazingly enough finding two nice hard seats.

About thirty seconds after I mentioned that we were going to have a very long wait, I heard Signora Colbourne called. Do you mean me? I indicated as I stood hesitantly, one hundred pairs of eyes boring through my body. "Si Signora, venire, venire". I rushed on behind the nurse, her purple clogs flying, her dark green coat billowing. How could it be my turn already? All these people were before me. Guiltily, I left them all behind as I was led through a maze of ancient corridors to Dottoressa Machiara. She was just as nice as she sounded on the phone. Seated at an old desk, the top of which was littered with files, papers, medical books, we exchanged introductions and she and Luigi spent at least ten minutes chatting about Canada and our house here in Italy. I was amazed at the office; a room filled to bursting with filing cabinets disgorging their tattered contents from over full drawers, piles of boxes, and books. The walls held notice boards covered with charts, graphs, notes, and cartoons. Vacant spaces on the walls announced that Pavarotti would be in Modena and that Verdi's Requiem Mass would be performed at Chiesa San something or other, and tacked between the posters was a recipe for walnut liqueur. There were handwritten notes pinned or stuck to every conceivable surface. The only indication of our presence in a modern day office was a computer, exhibiting the inevitable Windows program.

We went over my entire medical history, which had been faxed to Dr. Machiara from my oncologist. I answered numerous questions relating to the health of my siblings, mother, father, grandparents. Within this very small office circulated a constant flow of people, men and women, in white coats with stethoscopes, nurses in green and blue and white, people with masks. Some remained, leaning against file cabinets, curious it seemed, arms crossed. Others bent, elbows on the desk, looking at Dr. Machiara's constant scribbling. There was much conversation, discussion, and consultation. Was I really so important, or odd, that I could generate this much interest?

Finally released, to be weighed on a scale from the dark ages, and to leave a little blood for analysis, I was told to return in an hour and we made our escape. I was desperate for a cappuccino so we made a beeline for the coffee bar and staff canteen, outside across the parking lot. With not one space available on the baking tarmac we were glad we had left the car under the trees on via E. Coli.

It appears to me that the Italian government sinks more health dollars (lire) into hospital canteens than into medical equipment. "State of the Art" met us in every direction. Gorgeous chairs and tables, soothing dimmed lighting, washrooms from heaven, the bar lined with bottles of every aperitif imaginable, miles and miles of the most stupendous array of food, fruit, vegetables, bread, rolls, cheeses, every kind of hot pasta dish known to mankind. For staff, a plastic card slid through the till supplied a sumptuous feast for two thousand lire, about two dollars. For visitors, why stop at a cappuccino? Enjoy the same glorious fare for about eight dollars each, after all it was lunchtime and we were both ravenous. Floor to ceiling windows lined every wall providing views through the trees, across lawns, down shady avenues. In a central open-air patio with umbrella shaded tables, sit the coffee drinkers, smoking, and with the standard Italian ear growth, cell phones, sprouting from their heads. We enjoyed our superb selections of pasta and salad, and stuffed to the gills, we returned to Oncology. Many of the people were still there, faces dull and unemotional, resigned to the long wait.

Once again ahead of the queue, I was called to the doctor's office. Occupied by two new doctors and a nurse, I was again questioned on my medical history. Confirming what this doctor was reading from Dr. Machiara's notes seemed a waste of time to me, but when in Rome……. Directed to lie on the examination bed and being very obvious that no-one intended to provide me with a cover, I whipped off my top and lay down. As the doctor examined me, I looked up at him and saw one of the most handsome men I have ever encountered. It did not seem to matter that he had thrust his hand down my pants and was poking around in my groin as I looked at Luigi, feigning a swoon of pleasure.

After dressing and being informed that my blood was good (I knew that), we were told to return next Wednesday for my treatment. I looked questioningly at Luigi.

"Why can't she have it today? She's already behind schedule," he said.

"No, No, this is the first consultation. Come back next week," said the doctor. They are all so charming and I was so tired, I could not be bothered to challenge and we left amid much handshaking, thanking and smiling.

It was almost five o'clock when we arrived at the cool haven of No. 17, Rovinaglia. To me, it was a day wasted even though I have been assured often in Canada that Italy leads the world in cancer treatment and research. I would just have to accept their way of doing things. Little knowing I would be in for more surprises the following week, we settled back into our sort-of-routine.

❈ ❈ ❈

Thursday dawned golden and beautiful. Still, after four summers, I felt a sense of expectation and awe as I opened the shutters and gazed at the view. The wonderful old flaking and warped shutters, through necessity, were gone now. Steel ones, an ugly dull gold color, doing nothing aesthetically for the house, replaced them, but did not detach from the beauty of the view. I was not here for their purchase and installation and had no choice in color. We left that to Roberto, who as usual did a wonderful job, I would get used to the color. The eldest of Meri's sons, he is willing to complete some of the more necessary jobs of maintenance during the winter, a quiet time on his land, fitting the odd job in between his shifts with the Italian State Railway.

Luigi had gone off to the town to do food shopping, his only addiction. He spends hours reading labels, checking contents, weight, to obtain the best deals, going from shop to shop to find the freshest vegetables. He was a chef for so many years, he just cannot give up his love of food and his concern for a healthy diet. I was glad to see him take over what I had always considered to be the bane of my existence. After work on Fridays, I would fly into one supermarket with my list. Always the same store, I could rush round blindfolded, I knew exactly where everything was. Damn the cost, get out and home and shove it all in the cupboards and fridge and collapse with a glass of wine. The only similarity to Friday afternoons now is the wine, and not only Fridays. The forced retirement, even at a terrible price, has its rewards.

While Luigi did his thing at the shops I sat on the balcony enjoying the silence and my morning coffee knowing that the afternoon would bring the straightening of the kitchen cabinets! I was perched on one of the old wood-wormy chairs, which were now brilliant yellow, and drew as much calmness into my reservoir as possible, knowing how I would need it later.

My "yellow phase" struck two years ago. It had its origins in the Healing Touch therapy sessions that I enjoyed while enduring rigorous chemo sessions. My therapist worked on the Chakra theory of color zones being representational of different areas of the body. Long ago I thought this stuff was bunk, but two books by Frederick Frank, The Zen of Seeing and The Awakened Eye, which have become two of the most meaningful books in my life, changed my mind. They led me along a path of discovery and awareness of my own life and the world around me. Exploring and learning more about Zen and its connection with my love of drawing opened my mind and eyes to a whole new way of thinking and seeing. Thus, I am far more tolerant of, and open minded to, alternate methods of healing.

In any event, the yellow thing came about because my therapist, with no knowledge of my condition other than that I had cancer, zeroed in on my liver, which was misbehaving badly. My healing color is yellow and she urged me to dress and paint and surround myself with yellow, to aid me on my way to better health. Everything I ever owned that was yellow came out of the closet, drawers, and storage and draped me, the table, the sofas and chairs. Paintings of sunflowers became the norm, and every wall was adorned with the bright yellow blooms. I painted the closet doors in my art room with a jungle of leaves and flowers and included every shade of yellow I could manufacture. And this yellow phase followed me to Italy. It was the year that my neighbors and the villagers would finally be convinced that I was totally mad.

Luigi has been a migraine sufferer for as long as I have known him. Over the years we have discovered certain triggers, one of which is the smell of paint. My attempt to find good, odorless paint in the little town with only two old-style hardware stores, was more difficult than I expected. Eventually, from the dusty, brown depths of one of these rickety old shops, the lady who ran the store produced my paint. She was learning to speak English and the scene seemed amusing to the other customers as I struggled in Italian and she in English. After turning over the preposterous amount of twenty-five thousand lire, about twenty dollars at that time, for a mere litre of the stuff, I was able to rush home and start my project.

I asked Luigi if he minded if I painted this, that or the other thing, considering they were originally his mother's possessions. I did not really heed his reply. I just wanted to make him feel important, that his contribution to the redecoration was worthwhile. I took the four old wood-wormy chairs outside. I found three gruesome old picture frames in a huge wooden chest in the cantina and added them to my collection. There were two elderly bedside cabinets that could not look any more hideous whatever I did to them. Out they went to join the crowd.

The sparse but constant parade of villagers along the top road always amused me, they did not disappoint me this day. I knew their eagle eyes would not miss a thing. Within ten minutes huge black clouds rolled in over the hills and down came the rain. Away scurried the villagers. Into the cantina went the chairs, frames, cabinets and me. The only light down there comes from two tiny grilled windows and the doorway, but that would not stop me. Having sanded the chairs earlier I started on them first. With their woven straw seats they were beginning to look pretty gorgeous dressed in yellow. A second coat and they were ready to make their glorious debut. The frustration of running out of paint at this point was eased as the rain stopped and the sun came out again. Holding the chairs by their straw seats I carried them outside one by one and placed them proudly on the flat rocks of our little piazza. In the daylight they were astounding. The yellow was the yellowest yellow I had ever seen, and a moment of, "Oh my God, did I really do that?" gripped me like a vice.

I do have a touch of defensive stubbornness. Looking up at the road and seeing two old biddies staring with looks of disbelief, immediately erased any doubts I may have had, I shouted up to them, "Aren't they gorgeous, don't you just love my chairs?" Shaking their heads they wandered away towards Brattesani and I knew it would only be a matter of minutes before the word was out.

Leaving the chairs in the sun I went to find Luigi. He was gossiping with Guilio in the garage. It is difficult stop the conversation of two Italian men in full swing, so I did not bother to interrupt, but sat on an old box to wait.

I love Guilio's old garage. There is not much vacant space. Racks of ancient tools, belts, chains and choppers, iron stove-top rings, distributor caps, paint brushes, oil cans, every mortal piece of hardware you can ever imagine that might be used on an old tractor, or baler, or farm vehicle. All this and more covered the walls and helped fill the shelves piled with old magazines, work gloves, different bits of wood and steel bars and pipes, boxes filled with nails and screws and washers, nuts and bolts, paint cans and spray bombs. On a small shelf in the corner sat the ever-talking television, an integral part of Italian life. On the bench, under the bench, on the floor, hanging from hooks and nails, baskets filled with chestnuts, walnuts, hazelnuts, and potatoes. Old cement bags stamped with the Portland Cement logo, sat in a dusty pile in one corner. Wooden chairs needing to be repaired or restored, were stacked, tangled in an unbelievable maze of legs and arms, backs and rungs. Underfoot were bits of bark, nutshells, sticks, old leather boots, laceless, holey-soled and dead, and dirt tracked in over the years which had disintegrated to a thick layer of dust. Amid all this sat the wood stove, accompanied by boxes of newspaper and kindling. King Giulio's domain—for the moment. I have, at times, seen six or seven people stuffed in to this incredible museum of one man's life. I do not know how they fit but they appear to be arranged in the same organized mayhem as the other contents.

My yellow chairs waited. I gave up on the two of them and walked back to the house. Not long afterwards, Luigi, followed by the cats, always looking for handouts, appeared round the corner of the house. He has known for years that I am somewhat different from the norm. He smiled kindly and knowing better than to be critical of my work, suggested that perhaps the chairs were a little bright. The cats, Bianca and Laila, however, made a beeline for them and each, settling on a chair, curled up in the sun. They may be color-blind but they are not stupid. Those two chairs became the cats' chairs and wherever they were placed, inside or out, more often than not, one at least, was occupied by a cat. I bought yellow cushions, I stood my huge nodding sunflowers inside and out.

When I offered to paint the church, Pierina, the lady with the key, only confirmed with her rolling eyeballs, that the "artista matta" was not getting anywhere near her church. I am sure she envisioned yellow pews, yellow walls, and campanile, as she madly made the sign of the cross and backed away up the lane, her stick legs clad in red, blue and purple, diamond plaid knee high socks, which she always wore regardless of the weather. I felt honored when she confirmed my membership in her "funny sock" society by presenting me with a pair of these long, colorful wooly wonders to keep my legs warm during the Canadian winters.

Pierina is a unique being in this little nucleus of Italian mountain folk. She was a nonconformist from childhood, and considered an oddball by her peers. She had no desire to have a boy friend, much less get married. She is considered to be quite mad by her family and others who know her, with the exception of a few old ladies. I find her to be perhaps one of the saner members of this insular community. She has a terrific sense of humor and we both enjoy long chats, animated as usual, but interesting. She has valid points of view, is well read, and always open to new ideas. She is Giulio's sister, living upstairs in her part of his family home, and the kitchen downstairs, her one tiny dark, ground level room, with only two little windows on the world. Her daily inside existence revolves around a wood cooking stove, preparing pitiful little meals, seated at her table eating alone. She secretly feeds the three cats, leaving scraps on her window ledge, for fear that Meri will find out she is spoiling them. Her evenings are spent stretched out on the standard hard wooden bench with only the company of a television perched high on the sideboard, Cyclops constantly watching. I cannot imagine how she has endured most of the past fifty winters and the majority of other days in this room. Cleaning the church, mass and market days, the occasional gossip session with a neighbor and perhaps a visit to her nephew in the town have been her major events in life. Wandering the woods looking for sticks for kindling, gathering mushrooms, and sometimes raking hay make up the remainder of her life. A long-standing intense mutual dislike of each other has resulted in Pierina never being invited to, nor wanting to, attend Meri's family dinners. It is evident that our visits and those of Gloria and her family, help to provide Pierina with the stimulus she needs to continue, plus the fact that she and Giuliana get on well together. Pierina's sense of humor can erupt at a moments notice, transforming her face from a lifeless mask to a cheery look of sunshine. She is seventy-five now, so proud of her years. She will tell you that she speaks five languages and proceeds to reel off "I love you" in English, French, German, Spanish and Italian. She will describe the perfect man for whom she says she still searches. When Pierina chats with Luigi about the "old days" and they laugh a great deal, I enjoy watching her react and come alive. I have become quite protective of Pierina and defend her against criticism, refusing to listen. I will walk away from anyone who chooses to malign her. The bad feeling between some of those old cronies has been going on for years. Who am I to say who is right, wrong, or just wacky! I always side with the underdog and Pierina, to me at least, in this little corner of Rovinaglia, is the underdog.

Luigi arrived back with the groceries and I felt no guilt that I had spent two hours doing absolutely nothing. No time of peace and rest is ever wasted for me. I am an expert at doing nothing. This life in the village is so conducive to achieving that goal, at least for me.

We unpacked the groceries and "Leonardo" presented me with two concrete chisels and a mallet and the suggestion that I might like to play around with the plaster walls and see what was underneath. I cannot recall ever in my wildest dreams saying that I would like to chip off years of layers of plaster and paint from the inside walls, to expose the original dry rock construction. Luigi may have a memory like an elephant but I refuse to admit ever suggesting anything of the sort, but secretly I am excited by the thought. Knowing the signing of the documents was coming soon, I did not feel quite so reluctant to begin major renovations.

I began my rock exposure career as quietly as possible, not wanting to disturb the neighbors. Eventually I gave up that silly idea and chiseled and banged away without consideration for Pepino or Lena next door; never wearing her hearing aid, Lena would not have heard anyway. One cannot chisel quietly! I just hoped I could proceed in my own methodical fashion and would not be urged to finish quickly according to "Leonardo's" method of operation. After lunch he was too busy with the cabinets and then once again under the sink, to notice me and my chisel.

I proceeded in as orderly a fashion as possible starting at a top corner, intending to work across and down. Every bang from the hammer brought a shower of sooty crumbly lumps down from behind the beam. When part of a mouse's nest appeared in the corner of the sitting/dining room, I decided to stuff up that corner with cement because I did not want to evict the poor little thing. Later, however, with all the vibration the cement fell out anyway, so I just had to hope the little mouse was a brave fellow and could hang on for dear life when necessary. I was slowly progressing and becoming braver and braver, I removed inch thick slabs of concrete and plaster. The excitement mounted as each piece fell and another beautiful rock face was revealed. "Watch out Leonardo, Michelangelo is coming," I called, as grunts and groans slithered out from beneath the kitchen sink.

This original rock wall had remained upright and intact simply by the weight of one huge rock upon another. Small pieces of thin flat rock were symmetrically placed sometimes upright and sometimes horizontally in the spaces between. A dry clayey earth mixture called living clay, according to the expert at the monastery, was also used to tighten loosened stones.

I became so engrossed in my work that it was Luigi's turn to call a halt to the proceedings. The chair (no Workers' Compensation Board here) on which I stood was up to its rungs in a pile of rubble. The old work clothes I had first worn were lost somewhere in the mess as, sweating like a pig, I had stripped them all off. As Pierina entered for a look-see, she was amused at the spectacle before her of a woman clad in a now filthy t-shirt, Haynes-Her-Way undies, old hiking boots, with a mask now glued to a grimy face, balancing on a bright yellow chair. It was certainly worth a laugh.

The following day I continued to diligently chip away with my lovely new tools, now working in the kitchen. The bathroom door was crooked. I was quite determined to chip enough around the bathroom door to push it in on one side; I like everything to be straight. I did such a wonderful job with the chipping and straightening. I then mixed some cement to keep the door in place. Unfortunately that evening Leonardo was re-attaching the lock opening and suddenly, with an earth shattering crash, out came the whole lot from the wall with my pride certainly going before a fall. I know now that I am not good with cement! Fortunately he was not crushed to death.

By now the new sink was in place, the cupboards straightened, and the new elbows placed in the chimney allowing the wood stove to be moved over a bit. I have to acknowledge here that the three-finger, four-finger method worked for the first time in living memory!

We proudly showed off our remodelled kitchen to Pierina and explained the theory behind revealing the lovely rock walls. I must give her the credit for being the only member of the older generation who could see any point at all in what we were attempting to achieve with our efforts to preserve the physical heritage of this lovely old cottage.

Joints and bones and muscles soothed in a hot bath, we were ready to celebrate another day of achievement with Eliza's pizza. As I sank into my wine I thought, enjoy it while you can, tomorrow is D-day. Meri had arranged a "board meeting" at Maria's Pizzaria on the Portello at noon. At last, papers to be signed, deals to be finalized. I could almost taste it now. We were so, so close. I woke and slept and woke and slept that night, imagining all the hitches that might occur, all the things that might go wrong. I fantasized about how I would stomp out of the meeting, come home and pack and throw my love for Emilia out the window. Lord, what a night it had been. The deeds to No. 17 awaited.

After that memorable luncheon meeting which amazingly proceeded without a hitch, we returned with wads of papers and surveyors diagrams. The moment of realization that No. 17, Rovinaglia was now ours was almost overpowering as we walked into the house. The experience was like a new beginning. The walls, windows, the chestnut beams, the old wood stove, all took on a new, fresh, lively tone. The kitchen table sparkled in the afternoon sunlight which squeezed through the door behind us, the pot of flowers shone, as though in a spotlight. There was a lot of love left in the old girl and we were ready to reciprocate with our love for her.

I remembered all the "quiet" renovations we had tried to perform, all the new items for the kitchen and sitting room that we had tried to sneak in. I wondered how paranoid I, myself had become — had I been here too long?

What doubts I had were dispelled the next day when the postman came into the kitchen and flung his arms round us both in huge enthusiasm. Thrusting the electric bill into my hand, he said he would miss popping in to see how we were advancing with our work because surely soon we would get a mailbox. He said he knew Nona would approve and he reminisced about her years here and the difficulties she endured during the winters. We enjoyed him a lot and reminded him that he was always welcome to pop in for reno updates.

Each day now that we remained here would take on a different meaning, a different feeling. A feeling of actually belonging and being part of this little village, this little piece of Emilia! We behaved differently with each other. We were not both always right; we found room to accept each other's ideas on painting, renovation. I felt a real connection with the villagers, they no longer skulked by but called out gaily, sometimes even coming to the door to chat. But I still would not hang out the washing on Sunday.

❊ ❊ ❊

Pick a century to which we wished to return and we could drop ourselves into it with a one or two hour drive in any direction. There was no pressure to complete changes now. We could venture out on our rides of discovery with open hearts, with no doubts or misgivings about what our futures would be with No. 17. And so we began our celebratory trip intending to have a lovely dinner out. We chose Bardi, a one and a half-hour white-knuckle drive away. Bardi's 10th century castle stands dramatically atop a high rocky outcrop making the castle so impressive as it looms over the valley far below. The solid rock forms the foundations of the high dominant walls so cool and deep within, blocks of ice were carted in during the long-ago winters to maintain year-round refrigeration. Gathered within the walls protective embrace is the old town. Outside, spilling down the hillside spreads progress, the more recent construction of apartments and modern homes, paling in significance to this great castle

We strolled around Bardi and found new little hidden gems, tiny houses hidden in alleys, wonderful balconies and hidden gardens.

I always manage to find somewhere peaceful to sit and draw and more often than not, no interest in me, or my work is evident. I chose to sit at an outside café shaded with a huge hanging vine over a trellis. Enchanted with the church across the piazza I became very involved with my pencils and the feelings of the church and while the atmosphere seeps into my veins and heart to be ever remembered I am most often unaware of human presence. On this day, however, I felt a pair of eyes and for some time I resisted the urge to turn and establish their owner. When I finally succumbed, I must have unconsciously issued an invitation. An elderly man, thin and elegant in stature, a beret perched on his head and bearing down on a walking stick came and stood at my table. Something in me sensed he was an artist and he proved to be just that! He addressed me in German, which is often the case in Europe with people who meet me for the first time believing my height and coloring to be Germanic. Having eliminated that possibility when his comments drew little response from me and giving me no chance to indicate my nationality, he

tried French and something I believed to be Dutch. In the
politest way possible, I smiled and raised my hand in a gesture for him to stop. I explained in my best Italian that I was
visiting from Canada, that we were staying near Borgotaro
and asked if he spoke English. In perfect English he said
that he had been watching me for some time, that he was an
artist also and that if I walked round behind the café across
the square and on down to the park, I would have a perfect
view of "his" beautiful castle. I told him that I had drawn it
several times before. He said that no one would be able to
paint Castello di Bardi enough times to do it justice. His enthusiasm was so overpowering I felt seduced by his passion.
He described how every hour of every day, every season,
gave a different light. Every alleyway or hillside presented
another perspective of the castle. As he escorted me in a
wonderfully old-world gentlemanly fashion, his hand at my
elbow, we walked to one of the perfect views of "his" castle.
He did not tell me his name or what medium he worked in,
only that he had lived in Bardi for many years. As a younger
man he had traveled this way and promised himself, having
fallen in love with "his" castle, that he would one-day return.
He settled me in the perfect position, suggested that I devote
my life to my work as he had done, and bid me a gracious
goodbye, touching his beret and bowing slightly. My heart
fluttered and I felt sorry that he was leaving. Watching him
walk away down the road and across the square, a sense of
desperation came over me for I felt I could learn so much
from him. Would I ever have the good fortune to meet him
again?

Not long afterwards Luigi came wandering along, gelatto
in hand, having done his exploring thing. I selfishly thought
how glad I was that Luigi had not met the old man. He loves
to talk and would have monopolized the conversation and I
would never have experienced my little bit of special time
with this lovely old gentleman, "un uomo vecchio". We decided to return to the café by the church for our late lunch

and enjoyed our special celebration of ownership of No. 17, Rovinaglia, with beautiful pasta and melanzane, cheese and fruit plus a bottle of Merlot.

I must have a thing with old men because on a trip to San Secondo, I crossed paths with another elderly man. Our visit to San Secondo was not by chance. We had driven to Parma airport to pick up my sister-in-law, Annette, coming from London for a two-week stay. Her flight had been delayed for six hours, and while she sat knitting in Milan we wove ourselves another wonderful experience in and out of the alleys and buildings of San Secondo, and the remains of the 16th century castle. The north wing and the tower, which is used as the town hall, are all that remain of the original castle.

With the Year 2000 looming on the horizon, a huge renovation effort was undertaken several years ago to restore many of Italy's historical sites. The preservation and restoration of buildings, like San Secondo, will afford many more generations the opportunity to look back into the lives of intellectuals, artisans, and aristocrats. The grounds are filled with ancient trees, outside beneath the walls, what once must have been a moat, stretches a deep grass filled channel.

We spent some time exploring the village, discovering a workshop where two women were working on restoration of canvases and other works of art. The intrepid man in my life, whom I have to admit is responsible for most of our interesting encounters and discoveries, did not hesitate to step inside and start inquiring about their work. In doing so, we were to discover that the younger woman working on the restoration of a particularly beautiful old canvas, had degrees in Archaeology, Sociology, Anthropology, and Fine Arts. She had more knowledge of ancient history and languages than I thought possible for a mind of one so young. The workshop also housed some wonderful pieces by a local artist for whom the other woman framed. The color and style were quite unique. The consistent theme of women with masses of glorious, waved and curly hair and enchanting faces full of emotion, particularly attracted me and I wanted to buy them all.

Using his natural Italian charm Luigi asked if they might be able to transcribe the inscriptions I had copied from the rock we found embedded in the wall of the house. We became quite obsessed with the origins of the engraved rock. Having no camera with which to take a picture, I tried to make a rubbing, which did not work well. I resorted to a drawn copy of the rock face and we would take it wherever we went hoping to encounter someone who might help interpret its meaning. The young lady in the little workshop looked thoughtfully at my rendition and she consulted some leather bound tomes. She suggested that some of the letters looked Greek but then could not reconcile other characters and numbers with those letters. We of course were hoping it was some ancient meaningful relic, like the Roman coin we had found in the pile of junk that is now the piazza. She thought it was probably a headstone but could not confirm that. I left them chatting and escaped to walk back to the castle.

As I strolled through the grounds I could occasionally hear a beautiful tenor voice drifting through the air and believed it to be a compact disc or someone with a radio. It was quite lovely and faded away as I entered a dark little circular stairwell. A cardboard handwritten notice advertising a show of work by local artisans piqued my curiosity. The stairs opened into a huge, long room. It might have been an eating hall centuries ago. I could imagine long trestle tables laden with platters of food. Men and women dressed in 16th century robes, minstrels circling, and hounds lying beneath the tables waiting for scraps. One wall was roped off and I could see salons beyond, through high open doors, with frescoed areas being restored. The hall itself contained a wonderful display of pottery, metal and stone sculptures, clay and earthenware tiles, and plaques, the materials used extracted from the earth, hillsides, and river beds of the area. Other than the young woman on duty, I was the only person present. Wandering through at my leisure I felt as though I was being allowed a private viewing of these beautiful pieces. In awe of this talent, and feeling my own abilities to be quite inadequate I left to find a place to sit and draw, perhaps to set to rest those feelings of inadequacy.

I noticed that two old men on even older bicycles had stopped, where they met, in front of the splendid archway entrance to the remains of the castle. I sat on an old wall nearby. As they chatted, I did a quick sketch, loving the atmosphere they had created just for me. Eventually they moved on and when I saw Luigi sitting at one of the little cafes across from the castle, I went to join him and had my cappuccino. Again I heard that beautiful tenor voice. Closer and closer it came, until along the road cycled one of the old

men on his bike singing his heart out. I must have visibly
swooned for he dismounted at our table and just as though
he knew it was my favorite, he sang an aria from La Boheme,
"Che Gelida Manina". I have often wanted to steal Andrea
Bocelli and have him sing for me forever as I sit at my kitchen
table looking out across the valley. But this old fellow was a
splendid second and I was very sorry when he finished. Bowing in gratitude to our applause, he cycled away across the
cobbles. Luigi asked the gang of middle aged men sitting at
the other tables, why they had not applauded. They all
laughed and one replied that they had been listening to it for
twenty years, and anyway the old guy was nuts.

I was so glad that I had been seized with the desire to draw
those two "uomini vecchi", one of whom would remain very
special to me. I had my little sketch, which comes alive for
me as I remember the lovely sound of his voice.

Sadly it was time to leave and after picking up our charge
at the airport we wound our way through a lively night-time
Parma, found the via Emilia and drove into our little lane at
midnight. The full moon, the aroma of the fields and syringa
produced a surrealistic atmosphere that could not be ignored.
Out came the wine and the chairs and we sat on the piazza,
the walnut leaves serenading us with their rustling in the
warm breeze. At this moment there was no where better to
be on earth. We sipped easily into Wednesday. Unfortunately,
as this would be a chemo day, we had to end this most pleasurable time and made our wobbly ways up to the house.

We have a resident Mr. Toad as big as a saucer. He often
sits in the corner of the bottom step leading up to the patio
and kitchen door and I warned Annette to step carefully.
She almost passed out when she saw him. The next morning
she went on a vain search for Mr. Toad (who had obviously
gone to earth for the day) and thus firmly believed her apparition was alcohol induced. She had also consumed several
glasses of wine when she saw the soldier ants marching down
the wall of her room one evening. As much as I assured her

that they were really there, she vowed never to have more Italian wine. When she had just gone to bed one evening, there issued from her room the screaming of a banshee. Seeing bits of feather and fluff moving between a beam and the wall in the corner of the room, cowering on the bed, Annette cried, "But I have had no wine this evening." I was able to reassure her that it was the mouse in the loft getting settled for the night.

After my sister-in-law's search for Mr. Toad, it was time to head off for a visit to the hospital. Surrounding my drugs in cooler packs and fitting them between all the paraphernalia I had hauled along last week, I certainly did not expect to be bringing it all back at the end of the day.

Arriving promptly for my ten o'clock appointment, I, that is Gabriella, was once again ushered into the doctor's office quite quickly, despite once more running the gauntlet of the eyeballs. I was in and out in a flash and then had my blood drawn. Completely unnecessary I tried to explain, monthly is appropriate, but it was not to be. I thus waited until the afternoon for my chemo and the delightful lunch in the glorious cafeteria became a regular event.

Having a leisurely walk down a shady tree-lined avenue, we came across an amazing spectacle, at least for naïve, country folk from Canada. Roaring down the quiet tree lined avenue came four police cars escorting a prison wagon. Carabinieri disgorged from the cars, Uzis ready, eyes everywhere. From the prison-cum-ambulance van a stretcher was pulled upon which lay a portly man, a stereotypical looking mafioso. Annette and I thought he must at least be the godfather! Not wanting to hang around in such a situation we removed ourselves quickly from firing range. I fully expected Luigi to march into the fray and ask all about it but he did not this time, much to my relief, although he loitered. That ever present urge to see something more, as with most Italians, they tend to congregate at accident sites, appearing curious about what might have happened to the poor victims.

Finding another way back because the avenue was now closed off, we returned to Oncology. I handed over all my medication and medical paraphernalia and was very sweetly informed that they would use their own lines and needles. After being infused the first time via a larger needle than I was used to I had a huge bruise at the needle site that stayed with me until we returned to Canada. No amount of asking the nurses to use my Canadian needles would change their minds. We had hauled all these supplies from Penticton to Parma for naught.

My mind was conditioned to the lovely open area with comfy lazy boy chemo chairs at home. Lots of windows and bright happy daylight. I was staggered at the condition of the chemo rooms. This particular room was a square off-white windowless box with three ordinary dull colored plastic padded chairs, one in which I sat. Three other patients were receiving their treatment dripping from glass bottles. They look amazed at my plastic drip bags of saline and my drugs, just as astonished at their appearance as I was at the archaic drip bottles. On one wall was a plain small table and leaning across it, seated on a wooden chair with her arm outstretched containing the intravenous line, was an elderly woman who had fallen asleep with her bald head resting on the table against her other arm. Another patient sat bolt upright in a hard plastic chair receiving his goods. Knowing how one can sit for three or four hours or even a whole day being infused, I could not imagine how these poor people endure such cold, unfeeling conditions. The only moments of sunshine arrived with the nurses, who though rushed off their feet circulating between several different treatment rooms, managed continual smiles and happiness.

I was surprised at how much control the patients had over their own intravenous lines and soon learned that I was allowed to regulate my own flow and when the time came, switch from saline to chemo, if there was no-one around to do it for me. Although the connections were different, I was

glad I had learned how to administer my own chemo if necessary. I had been worried about that aspect because all
procedures at home were so precise and sterile and secure.
There is never any danger of being given the wrong drug as
we are always asked to verify the computerized labels on the
bags. I noticed here, however, that names were just scrawled
on bottles with a felt pen. I was glad therefore, that I was the
only person with the very distinguishable Canadian intravenous bags.

Because of the value of my particular medication I was
reluctant to leave it at the hospital and always had the
problem, small though it was, of keeping it on ice, not easy in
the burning heat of a tiny car with no air conditioning. I was
always glad when the individual vials, which provided three
treatments, ran out because then we were free to roam the
city and not worry about getting home to the fridge.

Parma is a beautiful city. Its spacious elegance is due in part
to the Farnese family whose foresight in planning and devel-
opment left a legacy of beautiful parks and avenues and
accessible medieval areas. We discovered a beautiful park on
one sojourn from the hospital. A circular plan with a grand
palazzo at the meeting of several wide walking paths. In the
center is a lake and in the center of that an island where many
birds and water fowl make their homes. Swimming around in
the somewhat green murky water are turtles and fish and we
discovered that some of the original turtles were abandoned
by people who no longer wanted to have them as pets. Some
poor things struggle around with only three flippers or half a
nose. Perhaps they are territorial or perhaps there is a bigger
abandoned pet lurking in the depths, but it is all very pathetic
set against such a beautiful backdrop of green serenity.

Having put Parma on the map and developing a Duchy of
impressive political force in Europe, the Farneses' century
of rule came to an end in the 18th century when Elizabetta
assumed the throne of Spain, upon her marriage to Philip V
of Borbone. When Maria Luigia, wife of the Emperor

Napoleon arrived to rule the Duchy, at the time of his exile, she brought with her a dedication to the arts and a love of music, her passion, as it had been with her aunt Marie Antoinette. During her rule the opera house was constructed and so began Parma's dedication to the arts and culture. Maria Luigia's administrative abilities encouraged a thriving commercial center and her love of Violets, which have always been Parma's prize, established its famous perfume industry. Promotion of Parma ham, first produced in Roman times, created the region's main export, and the local cheese, parmigiano, which continues to appear on every Italian table, together with many around the world.

Later the opera house provided a venue for Guiseppe Verdi and a place of pilgrimage for opera buffs which exists to this day. During the warm, quiet evenings, the strains of music can often be heard floating across the squares and down the avenues from the open windows of apartments and houses, Parma is truly a city of music lovers.

Our experiences with Parma are always times of enjoyment. People-watching provides entertainment as we enjoy a plate of pasta at an outdoor restaurant. It is known as the city of bicycles as well as the city of music. Deference to cyclists is a way of life in Italy, even in the high traffic areas, no cutting off, no squeezing out. Unfortunately, pedestrians are shown no such courtesy. In Canada we are used to stopping to allow people to cross the street at lights or designated areas, however, we tend to treat cyclist with disdain, "Get off the road," we roar, "you don't pay taxes." At first by habit, in Italy we would show courtesy to pedestrians. They would almost fall down in catatonic fits of shock unused to such polite drivers, and the honking of horns behind us, as vehicles have to wait, is incredible. We soon learned when in Rome... to hell with the pedestrians.

As with many towns and cities in Italy, the old central areas are off limits to cars and provide a safe haven for those on foot. The tinkling of bicycle bells is constant as every manner of persons pass by atop their rattling steeds. Clattering by over the pebbles, go the people of Parma. The signorile, the beautiful people, perched in elegant manner, posture perfect, erect, silk skirts flowing above long brown legs, gold-sandled feet and painted toenails, gentry propelling old pedals, fingers dressed in gold, bracelets sparkling on wrists. Manes of rich blond tresses, chestnut, brunette, and copper framing calm, placid faces. Old wicker baskets filled with bread and poodles. Ancient, professorial men, lost in their worlds of music, science, riding by dressed in tweed jackets, pants cinched at the ankle with bicycle clips. Heads adorned with wild white hair and faces filled with lines of time and learning. Old leather saddles, creaking their way along the street. Students on their way to or from the university, harried and stressed, or late for class, flying by, baskets full of books, weaving an intricate path between the pedestrians and bicycles. Others, stopping to greet a friend, remaining steadfast and unaware of those rushing around and past. Young men about town, white shirt sleeves rolled up, jackets stuffed in baskets with briefcases, secure in the knowledge that Versace never yet designed a piece of clothing that creases, sockless feet in Gucci loafers. Mothers with small children stuck in the basket, pudgy little legs hanging over the front, or perched on a cushion on the crossbar with Papa. Young women sheathed in clinging lycra, bell bottoms coming the full circle here as well as in the new world. Brown midriffs bare, and tight revealing tank tops, cell phones pressed to ears, vital continual communication with friends, mothers, sisters. The latest in technology and fashion carried by on old faithful bicycles, painted pink with matching skirt guards, brown and rusty, polished and shiny. Nuns, billowing habits, now and then revealing a white knee, crucifixes swinging, head dresses floating behind clinging faithfully around faces, at peace.

As we sit at a café, we are intrigued with the elderly man sitting at the next table. Not a word has passed between him and the waiter. Provided with a newspaper, a bottle of wine, he awaits his first course and reads the newspaper. Upon its arrival the paper is refolded perfectly and set aside. Eating delicately he replaces his knife and fork after each mouthful and dabs his lips with his napkin. He savors each mouthful of wine and continues in complete silence as second and third courses are served. Two slices of melon arrive with his bill. With the hint of a smile, he enjoys his melon. Leaving his money on the table, he rises, tucks the paper under his arm and walks away, disappearing from view behind the Romanesque cathedral. Luigi's curiosity gets the better of him and upon inquiring about the elderly man, the waiter tells us that he comes everyday at the same time, sits at the same table, eats the same food and spending precisely two hours, he leaves at the same time every day. Luigi's ever curious nature prompts the waiter to tell him that he will gladly ask the boss for more information about the man. "Non, non faniente," (it does not matter) I say, kicking Luigi's shin beneath the table. "Respect the man's privacy, please," I tell him. The feeling that the man's patronage is timeless, is far more meaningful to me.

One of the oncology nurses had recommended that we visit what I now call the Chapel of Angels. It is a small church, squeezed into part of the old hospital, which now houses the archival center. We decided to walk; never believe an Italian when she says, "Oh, it is only a five minute walk, at most." Half an hour later we crawled like people from an arid desert into the beautiful cool haven of the chapel. It was astounding, with many pillars from which dripped cherubic faces, pudgy little arms and legs and beautiful wings, each one different and hewn from marble. The angelic frescoes were equally as beautiful and we lingered long in this cool, amazing sanctuary. Loathe to leave, we knew we had a long, hot walk back to the car.

❈ ❈ ❈

Parma lies on the Via Emilia, a life-line of immense historical significance. Originally a Roman road, it was devised by
Marcus Aemilius Lepidus in 187 B.C., to join the ancient
City of Piacenza to Rimini on the Adriatic coast, opening up
a major communications and trade route for the Roman empire. At that time Emilia and Romagna were separate regions,
linked only by the Via Emilia. For two thousand years they
retained their own distinct cultural personalities. For centuries Romagna was part of Rome, the people distinctly Roman
in nature, an aloof aristocratic race, reserved, proud, cultured,
and very unwilling to allow assimilation of non-Romans into
their society. Emilia was comprised of many small colonies
providing a more diverse population, considered plebian by
the Romans, her people were more open and natural, working a region of plains spread at the feet of the Appenines.

Despite the union of Emilia and Romagna in 1860, these
separate identities of character were never lost. However,
the unique blend of cultures, of art, architecture and history,
and Epicurean delights have complemented the areas. The
Via Emilia became the backbone of the Region, and continues to be a major factor in the economy of Emilia Romagna.

Exploring cities along its route such as Piacenza, Parma,
Modena, and Bologna will reveal the beauty and splendor of
different architectural styles. Romanesque cathedrals,
Byzantine and Baroche arcaded walls, towers, window forms,
brick, rock, stucco colored in every shade of ochre, sepia
yellows, bright and dull finishes, new and rich, old and
crumbling.

Venture off the Via Emilia and it is very likely that you will
become completely disoriented amongst all this beauty. Foot
travel along miles of arcaded walkways through the center
of a city such as Bologna, will aid in a complete loss of bear-
ings. City maps are essential if you are ever to find your car
again. Unless one has supreme navigational skills, becoming
lost in this or any other Italian city is very probable, but the
experience is always worthwhile. Even the city maps will

not always afford you the opportunity to find your way through a medieval maze of streets, or two way streets indicated on the map last year which will have since become a one way system, causing much confusion and chaos to tourists.

However, the intrepid Canadian is never deterred. We once drove straight down a no-entry street anyway, even mounting the wide, shady, sidewalk to the blessed relief of an elderly oncoming cyclist. His head twisting like an owl, he watched as we did an amazingly fast and accurate u-turn, considering the traffic and the Plane trees, and sped back past him in the correct direction, smiling sweetly as we did so. Having French license plates on our car made me feel a bit better. He probably thought, "Oh, those mad French," not knowing that we are Canadians. It is also helpful to be obviously foreign when arriving at the place where five roads converge at a round-about. Being trapped on the inside circle of three or four lanes of traffic, and clipping round and round at sixty kilometers per hour is great fun. Coming to a stop, somewhere in the bowels of Bologna on one of these circles, with a million honking horns behind us, Luigi emerged holding his hands out in a "We're lost" gesture. From nowhere appeared a policeman, out came the map stretched on the hood of the car and Luigi, in halting French asked for directions. A red lollipop sign was produced and the screaming, honking traffic was brought to a standstill as the policeman cleared a way though it all and we made our escape from the circle of hell.

Somewhere else in the world all roads lead to Rome but we have since discovered that in this part of the world, all roads lead to the Via Emilia. Asking for directions can be futile but ask for the Via Emilia and everyone knows exactly where it is and will point you immediately in the correct direction.

The journey back into the present has its eye openers and along this Roman road now dressed in tarmac, parade the prostitutes. Very often black, or of obviously non-Italian origin they stroll along knowing that their seductive yet innocent demeanors will entice customers. I wonder if their income provides the resources to dress and carry themselves with such class, or if they are schooled in the art of fashion and posture? When compared to the women who walk the streets of Vancouver, they are certainly, in my estimation at least, the most elegant and beautiful of their trade.

Once we are on the Via Emilia, no problem. We are bound to reach Parma, and thence home. Hopefully the sun is shining and we can establish East or West as the case may be. We have been known to head off in the wrong direction, and ten or fifteen kilometers down the road enter a lovely little village, but not the little village we should be entering.

On one of these occasions we pulled into a square in front of a church to turn around, deciding to stop for a cool break. We parked and went to look inside the church. The cleaning lady was sweeping away and Luigi began to ask her about the history of the church. Not saying a word she held her broom in two hands in front of her, almost in a defensive manner and rushed away through the door off to one side of the altar. A few minutes later a fellow appeared. The most unlikeliest looking priest, he wore a black leather jacket, a Polo sweater and blue jeans, packing a pistol in a holder on his hip. Behind him came a clone, both drop dead gorgeous and I twigged at that minute that they might be police. The questions began. Who were we? Did we have our passports? Why were we here? What I thought was absolute nonsense, went on for several minutes before Luigi was given the opportunity to explain the who, what and why. Their tense demeanor became a little relaxed as the clone explained that two "Albanese" had just made off with all the gold stuff from the altar. Come to think of it the altar did look a bit bare, dressed only in its pretty lace cover-up, and upon which stood a lonely looking Virgin Mary. Under their guidance and scrutiny we were allowed to look round, all the time being steered towards the door. These men, whom we discovered to be secret police, apologized profusely for their harsh attitude and hoped that it would do nothing to affect their reputation as law enforcers, or our appreciation of their beautiful Country. After we left we had a good chuckle and then debated, as always, the issue of the "Albanese," the Albanians.

I never win this discussion. Most Italians whom I know are strong in their belief that the Albanians are responsible for everything bad. Every robbery, assault, car theft is perpetrated by Albanians. It appears these crimes did not exist before the boats began arriving in Bari, bearing these illegal immigrants. Every street vendor is an Albanian selling stolen goods. Every panhandler is an Albanian sucking off society. I have heard it all before at home, where the seasonal influx of transitory fruit pickers into the valley are blamed for petty crimes committed during the picking seasons. Years ago in England, the "foreigners" of Latin decent were blamed for everything, every petty crime imaginable. Luigi himself, at that time a legitimate immigrant to England, was treated like dirt by employers, customers and strangers alike. He had to report to the police station every month with his immigration papers, as did all immigrants. If he did not, the local bobby would arrive at our house on his bicycle to check him out. I am still at a loss to understand this pathetic attitude towards the Albanians, most of whom are desperate to settle into a life of peace and hard work. Those thieves who robbed the church certainly did not leave their calling cards. I have heard many disrespectful remarks from enough Italians about the wealth of the churches to understand that anyone might be capable of such a crime, not necessarily the immigrants. Debating controversial topics with the Italians I know, is a waste of time; their minds are closed to anything but what they perceive to be the facts. What continues to amaze me is how I can fall so easily into the trap of a discussion, which quickly becomes a free for all, like a Canadian political debate. Woe is me, such a glutton for punishment. Familiar names begin to appear on road signs, as we head home once again, with yet another experience to store away for future retrieval in a Canadian winter.

Another memorable "lost" occasion occurred two years ago. We had strayed far from the Via Emilia out into the hot flat plains. We came to a village snuggled round the feet of a castle, and drove round for awhile trying to find somewhere shady and quiet to have our usual picnic. The castle was private and closed and the streets although shady offered no space to park. Luigi stopped an elderly man on his bicycle to ask if there might be a park somewhere close by where we could have our picnic. Without hesitation he shouted, "Venite con me," as he sped away on his bike. We followed along, at the speed of sound it seemed, amazed at how fast his little old legs were pedaling. Round the corner, down a narrow street, out through the archway of the city walls, down the little hill, through some poplars to a beautiful park stretched along the shore of the sparkling river. Tons of parking, and not a person in sight. Perfect! We beeped our thanks to the cyclist and began a leisurely hour of eating, paddling and poking around across the road through another archway in to the old town.

There are also those "losts" of stupidity. Men who refuse to take maps because they know the way! Men who drive round and round in circles, unable to admit they are lost, pride not allowing them to ask for directions. It has to be a man thing; I have heard so many women say they have had the same experiences. That is not to say women cannot get lost, but we have no hesitation in admitting it and asking for help or stopping to dig out the maps.

After reading an announcement in the paper about a Ferrari car show in a small town called Traversatolo, an hour or so away, according to the map that we did not need, which remained on the kitchen table, we left in high spirits. It became obvious to me after at least an hour on the road that we were lost. Surely the cartographer had not just popped the little black dot onto the map for fun, although I was beginning to wonder if the place existed. I suggested we stop and ask for directions, but no, we would still be able to find this elusive place. Having controlled my exasperation as we drove hither and thither, crisscrossing back and forth what seemed to be most of Northern Italy, I shut the pleasant-agreeable wife in the glove compartment and allowed the aggressive-impatient me to leap from the car as we drove slowly past a café. In my best Italian, I asked where was the Ferrari show? The magic word Ferrari unleashed a stream of incomprehensible directions from every young man at the café. Before Luigi had time to respond to my not so polite request to get out of the bloody car and come and talk to these bloody kids, a delightful young man mounted his gorgeous bright red motor bike and indicated we should follow him. We did, in atmospheric silence, heading out of the village and down a long straight road dividing beautiful fields of poppies and wild flowers and unmown grasses. In the distance I could see a wooded area. As we neared the trees the lovely boy pointed to a huge wrought iron gate and then zoomed away to be swallowed by the red poppy fields. We could now see a gravel area where some vehicles were parked so we stopped there.

Walking through the gorgeous great gates we came into the most beautiful grounds. Acres of green manicured parkland surrounded a beautiful villa. Huge cedars with trunks as big as houses spread their boughs of dark green in huge lacy fans layered round and up the monstrous trees. Beautiful rose gardens set out among little hedges. Statues of angels and Venuses and Davids and Gods and Goddesses were set here and there throughout the grounds. Peacocks and pea hens stepped softly and elegantly on the grass. White doves and mourning doves cooed in the trees and walked among the peacocks. It was all just too beautiful for words. In front of the great Villa Corte de Mamiano, lay a spectacle of scarlet red Ferraris, as elegant as the peacocks wandering among them. The whole scene appeared to present itself in slow motion. People walked slowly round the cars, stopping often to ponder over these beauties. Even the few children were composed and well behaved. It was all quite surreal. Sixty years of sleek, glistening, scarlet machines in complete harmony with the 18th century architectural beauty as their backdrop. I was in heaven.

Long before I attained the last name of Ferrari, I loved cars. My father was the first person on our street to have a car and he would take my friend and me for rides. I always felt so proud, sitting in the back seat like the queen. I would practice emulating Queen Mary, King George's mother, as she would be driven past the end of our street in her coach up to Cliveden. She would wave to the little people gathered along the way. I had that wave down pat. I cannot imagine what people thought as I graciously acknowledged my subjects. When my father had business at the local car dealership I would spend hours looking round the showroom. I knew every make and model on the roads. As I grew up my passion for cars continued and I dreamed of owning something sleek and fast. Lack of money, mortgages, children, common sense prevailed, until my sleek, black "midlife crisis" sat in my Canadian driveway. Unfortunately it did not sit there for long. I generously allowed a few select others to drive my gorgeous sports car. The last driver, my son, planted it firmly beneath a semi. My son was very contrite, but at the point of viewing the wreck, I was thankful the air bag had worked for him.

We spent a long time looking at the Ferraris. It seemed inappropriate to talk or make any noise as the other onlookers walked in worshipful manner among their scarlet gods. The Villa called us and we mounted the wide stone steps up to the area in front of the open doors, crossing the wide balcony stretched out to each side rimmed with an ornate marble balustrade. Statues stood here and there among huge potted oleanders and magnolias. From the huge vestibule, a circular marble stairway curved up from each side to the second floor level. In the center of the vestibule stood a massive stone font and I wondered how any priest could reach inside let alone pop a baby in to be baptized. Signs indicating a specific route to follow for a self-guided tour of the Villa sent us off through a high squared arch. Our next hour was spent in peaceful awe as we encountered several salons lined with beautiful 17th and 18th century paintings. We continued to roam through the villa and dream of what life must have been like for the residents of this beautiful place. I will often stroke walls or banisters as I explore these places, imagining the generations of those who went before me.

Time was passing too quickly and before we knew it was time to have lunch. Outside we looked for a place to have our picnic, finding several cool concrete benches surrounding an outdoor courtyard, where elegant people sat at tables set with linen and crystal, the Ferrari logo prominent on menus and napkins, these were the elite. They definitely would not ask the price of the car when they buy a Ferrari. Our humble picnic would not fit in among this lot so we slunk off into the grounds and enjoyed the company of glorious shimmering peacocks as we ate our torte d'erbe and focaccia.

Somewhat reluctantly we left this dreamlike place, driving home through the countryside, passing the old farm houses and beautiful villas at the end of long tree-lined driveways heralded by old pillars and huge iron gates or crumbling ancient archways. Many pillars are topped with the familiar "pineapple" a traditional sign of welcome. The little villages and towns were quiet, the afternoon shutdown in progress, benches occupied by the old folk watching the world pass by their doorsteps.

Driving through the Taro valley, we follow the same route each time but the opposite side of the valley always intrigues us. The ever present churches dot the hillsides, little red roofs, some in clusters, others lonely farm houses, disappear from view behind the hill crests into the numerous valleys that drop down to the river. We often plan to find a road across the river which we can follow to explore the villages on the other side of the valley, especially the old ruined castle that appears to stand alone on an island in the river. Someone, once upon a time, must have found a way over there. But of course, we have to save some adventures for other times.

❧ ❧ ❧

A great challenge is still to come as we begin our ascent up to Rovinaglia, the villagers' only lifeline to the world. I have driven thousands and thousands of miles all over Europe and North America but for several years I fully expected to pass from this world to the next on the road to Rovinaglia. Whenever I meet the milk truck or the garbage truck I imagine being dispensed to greener pastures as we both try to pass on a road only wide enough for one. Meeting, as always, on a tight precipitous bend, never on a straight stretch with a nice firm field to steer into, I can see myself hurtle away over the edge like Thelma and Louise. Hopefully on the way back from town, then at least I would have had my cappuccino. Over the years, as we made our first trip up the road each spring or summer, the pathetic repairs to the surface were evident. A mickey-mouse effort is all the "Lavori Pubblici" (the Public Works department) need to keep the villagers happy it seemed. The same men in their orange overalls fix the same potholes every spring. Their shovels dispense dobs of tarmac from the truck into each hole, pat it down and move onto the next one. By the time September rolls around the potholes have reappeared, grown and sprouted lots of babies nearby. Always starting at the bottom of the six-kilometer stretch of road, the budget seems to evaporate at km three and from there onwards continues the bone rattling obstacle course to the top. Negotiating the potholes is akin to running an obstacle course. Night driving is a fun filled experience trying to follow an unlit and unlined zig-zag through the black-as-pitch night. Knowing that the few guard rails so kindly installed eons ago have sunk below road level due to constant land erosion or have completely disappeared over a drop-off, adds to one's feeling of security and well-being! If the powers that be allot a few million more lire than usual, then the two men in their orange overalls will multiply by two. A more concentrated effort will then be made to shore up a few crumbling edges and add a bit more tarmac to small holes which might otherwise have been ignored. Some nice white lines will even be painted along the edges, below the winter fog level, of course, enabling drivers to see the edges at night. And, of course, repaving when it does occur runs out at km three with a distinct bump. We once suggested to one of the workers that should they ever reach Rovinaglia we would share a bottle of wine with them to celebrate. We also wondered if the Mayor lived at Km three.

Listening to the villagers complain about the condition of the last part of the road and listening to Guiliana ranting about the dangers of driving in the perpetual winter fog and not being able to see the edges of the road, we were at a loss to understand why they did not represent themselves at a council meeting and convey their concerns. "Oh, shoosh, shoosh, no, you can't do that," they would say. "The Communale would never listen. They would stop garbage collection up here. They would send spies to catch us chopping trees or picking mushrooms. Oh no, no, we don't want any trouble." I almost expected someone to suggest they did not want to have to pay protection money. All this paranoia exhibited by the villagers was so alien to us. The city council are just people, like them, no better, no worse. Our frustration at their attitudes led us to an interesting encounter with "the powers that be" at City Hall. We decided one day to drop into the town hall and found the mayor's office up many flights of stairs and through dark dreary hallways. Luigi's theory was if you can drop by to see our mayor at home then why not in Borgotaro. Why not indeed?

Penetrating the inner sanctum proved to be somewhat akin

to breaking down the city walls. An hour-long wait, spiced with wars of words with several different minions and lesser souls, resulted in penetrating the protective wall of the mayor's secretary's office. Another polite but lengthy discussion with the secretary, explaining the situation went on and on. Undaunted, Luigi pressed on with his polite but insistent demands. We never did establish the breakthrough point, but visibly deflated, the secretary finally phoned into the Mayor's office and Luigi was admitted to the big man's inner sanctum.

Does the mayor live on the Rovinaglia road? No he does not. Has he ever driven the road? No he has not. Does he even know such a place exists? Well, yes of course he does, but he is a busy man. He has a budget with which to work, and there is so much infrastructure within the town to be maintained and repaired, where will he find the money to repair the Rovinaglia road? "The same place you found it to pave the road all the way to Albaretto," a wealthy little community on the other side of the hill from Rovinaglia, suggests Luigi. "The same place you found it to pave the road up to San Vincenzo church." (The church where the priest lives). A promise to drive up to Rovinaglia was extracted from the Mayor and we left. Doubting that he would ever follow through, we were quite prepared to make a few visits to his office until something was done. We never told anyone about our little crusade for fear of unleashing the wrath of goddess Meri upon our shoulders, but a few days later, much to our surprise, a small bus was seen in the area. Important looking men in suits exited, stood, looked, re-boarded and left. The word was out. The stories, fed and nourished by the villagers' outrageous ideas about what this all meant. Someone said they even saw an Uzi disguised beneath a long black trench coat! It could not get more ridiculous but we kept quiet and enjoyed the different stories. I wondered how long it would take for this story to grow beyond all comparison, how many versions might be created in the minds of the villagers?

Within a week, the work crews were out. Starting this time at the church, they worked their way down the road. By the time we left in August the repairs were almost completed. Except for one hazardous corner known for the last hundred years as "la cava", the quarry, because the whole corner just drops away into a precipitous rock fall. The road to Rovinaglia was repaired, if not repaved, being somewhat smoother and safer to negotiate. The white side lines were, however, only completed to the San Vincenzo turn-off, which of course gave our beautiful niece the wonderful opportunity to complain again about how useless the City was, because from there to Rovinaglia, the last two kilometers is where the winter fog is like pea soup. Of course, the paint crews did it deliberately to irk her. She works at the Justice of the Peace office, so she should know.

A stop at the flower shop was in order as Luigi made a trip to town about two weeks later. I am sure he felt a twinge of guilt as he presented a lovely bouquet to the women in the town hall office. He thought he had been a bit hard on them but whether he had or not, the flowers generated lots of happiness. The orange-overalled workmen are still waiting for their wine. A similar situation occurred two years ago when Luigi was applying for the necessary papers to buy a car. The rigmarole, red tape, and attitudes of one or two people were somewhat annoying. To calm the troubled waters, he returned the next day with flowers. From then on, business conducted in that particular department has been a breeze. Flowers are a cheap and legal form of bribery! A way of life in Italy that still exists despite vehement denials from those on the receiving end. In any event the lifeline to the outside world continues to be quite well maintained.

The end of our holiday approached. A hitch had occurred with the document signing for the land. When the papers were submitted to the City Hall, confusion arose as to why Nona's name was still on the tax role. Also Roberto had the bright idea that if his brothers' and sister's names were also included on the documents, the taxes would be split six ways on the land. A good idea, but why had no one thought of it before? Off we went back to Canada, owning the lovely little house, but still no land on which to step from the bottom of the patio stairs.

Chapter VII

2001

The coffee was tepid and the snack was a ham sandwich to which I succumbed, my strong vegetarian principles going by the wayside, I was hungry. We were sitting on hard chairs in a freezing cold parkade for what seemed like hours. Tarps hung from the concrete ceiling and between each concrete pillar, billowing in the cold wind, and as far as the eye could see there were hundreds of people sectioned into groups of about sixty or seventy, waiting patiently for their flights out of Heathrow. Our return trip to Canada had been snarled and complicated by the tragedy in New York on September 11, 2001. Having been delayed because Canadian and United States air space was closed, we had been rescued by my brother and stayed in Kent for five days awaiting available seats. Now the attendants were handing out blankets and I greedily took two and made a pillow with one, which I stuck behind my freezing, bald head against a pillar. I achieved some degree of relaxation, shutting my eyes and picturing my beautiful Emilia. If all the pictures, photos, drawings, postcards were piled up and burned, nothing could ever destroy the rich images in my mind of Emilia's beauty and grace, people and architecture, her rolling fields of scarlet poppies and wild flowers, the power of her gorgeous mountains and the grandeur of the Po, winding its way at first quietly then hugely through Emilia, my forever love. I drifted back to that moment in time two months earlier, when we arrived in Italy for what has become almost a yearly pilgrimage.

My heart is huge, full of emotion and love as once more I crawl out of bed and head for the window. I hesitate, savoring that first moment of joy as Emilia reveals herself. I know this love I feel is rich and enduring and I quaver inside wishing that it would never end. The sky is gray as the marino fog drapes its soft clouds over the Tuscan ridge and fingers of gray fall gently down onto Emilia. A small cotton wool band of clouds lifts to reveal the horizon, the familiar lemon light of the early sun steals through, some of the tree-tops are touched by its rays. This first wonderful view of Emilia from the bedroom window always banishes the misery of the previous day's long journey and midnight arrival. Just at this moment the seven o'clock bells ring out across the valley in welcome. The chickens are already out clucking and gossiping in the grass below like the old ladies on the balcony. Oh it feels so good to be back.

After a very difficult five months having had a brain tumor removed and long recovery period of tottering around with a cane, this is what I need to renew the peace and tranquility of our lives. My brother refers to our house in Canada as "Tranquility Base #1", and now after his first visit to the peace and beauty of the Italian countryside, our little Italian house has become "Tranquility Base #2". He and his family live at the intersection of five roads in what is now London but once was Kentish Country, so anything might seem tranquil compared with the buses and cars and emergency vehicles roaring hither and thither in front of their house.

Wrenching myself from the view, it was time to inspect the house. We knew that the winter had been three months of non-stop rain here in Rovinaglia, and the whole of Northern Italy had suffered devastating floods. We were prepared for the worst as Rosetta had said the walls and ceiling were covered in black mossy mold; the mice had chewed on most of the linen and pooped everywhere. In fact she and her daughter, Lorena, had done a wonderful job of cleaning. The kitchen had a half black, moldy ceiling, the beams were just as bad and the interior walls with outsides fully exposed to the elements were a white with black moldy polka dots all over the inner surfaces. The wood stove had rusted into a lump of steel grunge, where the runnels of water had leaked down the outer surface of the flu and settled on the surface of the stove. It could be worse, at least the house had not been swept down the hillside as had happened in so many hill towns that winter. That afternoon we set to scrubbing off as much mold as possible. Several cans of paint were necessary to complete the clean-up. After a week working a little at a time, the house looks absolutely gorgeous again.

My dear little Italian house—how I missed you. I did notice while repainting that the kitchen cupboard has loosened its hold on the wall, clinging to life on two loose brackets, but I could not face that job so I think I will wait for Luigi to notice it himself. Hopefully it will wait until next year to fall down. I decided not to drape the windowsills and railing with geraniums as every year previously they have been mangled and destroyed by the wind. Looking at the bare windowsill and railings, the flat rocks around the flower garden where I usually place the pots, I felt sad that the house would not be a riot of red this year. Waving gently in the breeze I could see the little group of "Jennifer's" poppies squeezing up between the flat rocks of the piazza, little faces smiling up at me, so my senses were somewhat soothed. I knew it would not be long before Luigi and his yellow machine would be out desecrating the landscape, so I made a point or two or three, of reminding him to circuit the poppies, and he did, and they were still holding onto life when we left in September.

Having no strength is very frustrating; I hate asking Luigi to move this rock or that slab. I think he plays a game with me knowing I cannot do it. He ends up landscaping his way, which of course is fine; it always ends up looking lovely although contrary to my original vision. He really is an inveterate rock man. All the pieces, whatever the shapes, fit together as if in a puzzle. To me it could all remain a jungle and I would just snuggle down in the middle and love it all forever.

I thought it would be nice to remodel the roof of the porch, making it more in keeping with the style of the house. The old barn down at Banshoele, Luigi's favorite piece of land, has some wonderful old tiles that have fallen in, perfect to remodel and roof the veranda, but how to get them through the tangled jungle and up the hill through Primrose Lane presents a problem. At present there is an ugly piece of white, ridged corrugated perspex over the kitchen door, which serves as rain run-off, but not much else. It seems simple to me to take that off, bolt a sheet of sturdy plywood to the iron frame, extend it one or two feet each side and front to provide a more efficient shield against sun, wind, rain and whatever else gets thrown at the kitchen door, and then tile that to match the roof. But Roberto keeps advising against this because of safety aspects. Luigi will not ask for help to bring up the tiles and I can see five years from now, after five hundred wheelbarrow loads, I might get my tiles.

I thought we might employ the "Tractor Boy", Sylvano, a quiet, handsome young man who is always out and about on his tractor, a saucy little dog leading the way, to haul up the tiles. Since we have been coming here, his mom, who came from England as a teenager, appears to be a very sad lady. She invited me for tea one day, obviously lonely, she talked a lot and I felt a strong underlying current of misery as she related the aspects of her life in Italy. I tried to be sympathetic, but selfishly did not want to counsel and be a friend, and so I did not go again. She has recently had a baby; perhaps this has made her happier. Sylvano is much happier too. I see her sometimes and we wave and have the odd word together. She certainly appears to be happier and for that, I am very glad.

I know Roberto has nixed the idea of a tiled roof because he says the wind will blow the tiles off in the winter; well we do now, thanks to the "Land Baron", have insurance, so when the tiles fly straight through his window we will be covered!

He was here this year, the "Land Baron"! He and his wife

come to Rovinaglia each summer from London. Perhaps some of my animosity is rooted in stories I have heard from Luigi about the "Land Baron's" father, about his siblings. The father spoiled them all, they never had to work on the land or help their mother. The family was very wealthy and I think I can understand how Luigi and his sisters must have felt at that time. I hear his familiar whistle and, looking up from my coffee to see him at the top of the path, he greets me with his usual "Good morning madam, how are you today?" So very English with his white undershirt! Always hanging out the laundry or performing domestic jobs to help his wife, more English now than Italian; I find this admirable and he is a nice enough person, but he gets under my skin. He always knows best, he is always right! "Get insurance, pave the driveway, put up a safety fence, secure those tiles…." I try to keep the chat brief because I know he will soon launch into all the wrongs he has been done by his scheming cousins with land deals and fences placed two inches onto his property and, on and on. Oh dear, I just want to sit on my porch and be left alone. I like positive people, and yet here in Rovinaglia they are mostly hard-done-by. Well it is early in our holiday—I will soon be trying to perk them all up and telling them how lucky they are. Of course at this point none of us knew what was going to happen on September 11th. I think the villagers all had a good shake in their shoes and perhaps learned to appreciate what they have, to stop complaining about the petty things in life and learn to enjoy each day as a gift.

We spent much time painting and cleaning and tidying up the garden we felt like a change of scene, so the following week we headed off to the seaside in great spirits, contemplating the wonders of the Mediterranean coast. We had discovered the beach at Marina di Carrara last year. I have to have sand and sun and salt water if I am within smelling distance. Every time those marine mists crawl across the hill-tops from Liguria, I can almost smell the salt crystals.

Unfortunately the bad winter had caused several landslides across the Tarodine valley, a huge amount of earth and trees had slid from atop their rock base, passing so close to two old homes it was a miracle they were not swept into the river amid the mud, rocks and trees. I suppose it might take a few years to regenerate the land with deciduous trees and brush but the beautiful fir trees are gone for a very long time. Another huge slide on the Bratello pass to Pontremoli caused weeks of long detours via the autostrada. Now there is a man-made detour around the slide and travelers are once again able to go over the pass to the coast. Hating the autostrada as I do, we took the longer route, the wheels spinning, throwing rocks and gravel, as we braved the precipitous detour, then on over the Bratello pass, down through Pontremoli and on along miles and miles of winding wonderful country roads. Changes in vegetation took us among hedges of oleander, white, pink, red and mauve; the tall waving reeds with corn like leaves that thrive nearer the coast, and of course, bougainvillea. Every balcony was draped in rich healthy geraniums. Churches and villages, and outside-cafes, markets and little old people sitting by their doors with toes in danger of being crushed by our wheels, slipped by. Then on through the fields of sunflowers and there, oh, there she is, the shimmering sea waiting just for me.

It was hot, very hot, as we drove along the road parallel to the beach. The foresight of the local government restricting the construction of large hotels, apartment blocks and residential homes on the sea-side of the road, made this area a very pleasant and less busy sea-side community than the teeming throngs that choked other resorts.

We parked amid the oleander bushes across from the public beach, a huge, clean, well-maintained area with a cappuccino bar, clean washrooms and showers. We crossed the busy road, clutching our beach paraphernalia, the brolly, chairs, tote bags with towels and water and buns and cheese, books and drawing stuff of course, ready for our lazy day. The array of umbrellas along the sand was spectacular. The colors, designs, the swaying fringes and ribs holding towels, and sun dresses in a further splash of color, set against the magnificent blue water and sky. By the time I had sucked in all the splendor of the color, Luigi found a nice spot. I spread out the old Italian blankets as far as I dare to secure the largest area possible so I would not have to be near other people and have to talk! Of course Luigi makes up for it because he talks to everybody anyway. As the Director of Beach Trips continued to organize, I could wait no longer to enter the enticing Mediterranean. I tottered on one good leg and one wobbly leg to the curling, frothy waves. I tried to step in carefully but the waves tossed me in unceremoniously. Gagging and choking on the salty brine, I managed to right myself and swam joyously out and then parallel with the beach. As usual I was overcome with awe at the sight of the marble mountains forming a huge white backdrop to this coastline. I thought about how Michelangelo had chiseled his way though the marble with his trainees and helpers, creating David, the tombs of the Medici Princes, the Pieta, and so many more wonderful sculptures. We take all these things for granted, but their tools must have been so limited by today's standards, their efforts, I am sure, staggering.

Trying to get out of the water was fun. Swept off my feet here, thrown in a dip there, dragged back by waves, then swept in again, I made a dash for freedom on my hands and knees, collapsing on the sand. I looked up to see the beach people staring at this apparition before them. A baldheaded beanpole, now standing, though wobbly. Great entertainment, I laughed; the spell broken, they joined in this moment of humor. Collapsing finally beneath our umbrella, Luigi thinking he might have to soon check my vital signs, rushed off to find cappuccino. Watching him approach, I noticed the proper china cup and saucer, not the usual styrofoam cup.

"Si, va bene, poi portare una tazza di cappuccino per tua moglia nella spiagga." "Yes, yes," the proprietor had said, "take the nice cup of cappuccino to your wife on the beach." Revived now with this caffeine dose, I walked back up to the café, returned the cup with great thanks and continued on across the road to look at the little booth-style shops selling all manner of beach accessories. I picked through the sundresses, tiny, cotton, skimpy things, and made my decision then to transform my garb from the shorts and t-shirt of a Canadian tourist to an Italian beach-goer. The bikinis were tempting but I was not inclined to compete with the beautiful bronzed bountiful bosoms on the beach. Oh that cursed flat English chest. On reflection perhaps, I should have been brave, for after our return home, I was diagnosed with another type of breast cancer. I ended up with half a chest as I lost a breast to the new tumor. Definitely no bikini next year! Images of a prosthetic breast floating away across the Mediterranean are quite amusing though.

The usual, mostly African, hawkers prowled the beach with their wares; balloons, blankets, kites, toys, towels, hats, sundresses, shorts, cameras, jewelry, watches, tons of stuff, none of which interested most people. A polite "non grazie" was usually enough to send them on their way. If a man was insistent, he was treated to Luigi's inquiring mind and was bound to answer all his questions. Many of these people had walked from distant points in Africa to Morocco where they spent months living on the streets and beaches of Tangier hoping to board boats sailing up into the Mediterranean. I cannot imagine how awful life must have been for them to undertake such an epic journey. These people migrate inland after the summer. We encountered them as they wandered with big sports bags on their shoulders, laden with wares. We were in Tornolo one day, Luigi off on his bike and I looking for interesting things to draw, among the medieval homes and along the cobbled alleyways. I decided on a 12th century house that appeared uninhabited, except for the geraniums pouring down the steps. Engrossed in my very meditative exercise, I was approached by a Moroccan man with his huge blue bag of wares, stinking of every type of cologne you could possibly mix together, which wafted its insulting way down those quiet unassuming lanes. The salesman was at work, and I tried to ignore him but he kept on about my drawing, and pestered and pestered. I finally had to be quite forceful and say "No, I do not want to buy anything, please leave me alone." Well If I had spoken perfect Italian that is what I would have said, but after several no thank you's, I had to resort to the rude, abrupt "via, via;" "get out of here." I watched as he approached his next potential customer, an old man, perhaps seventy-five or eighty, dressed in the usual village garb, baggy old pants held up by braces, a rolled-sleeved, frayed-collared, striped shirt. His grizzled chin clasped in his hand, he leaned against a wall. He listened intently with feigned interest. "Of course you need a real Gucci watch, look how handsome that would look on your brown hairy wrist, and here, smell this, how it will charm your wife or your girlfriend. Perhaps you would like this lovely silk bandana to tuck into your shirt collar, look, just like this. Or maybe you should get a nice new table cloth and napkins for your wife." I could see the game being played out and although feeling a little sorry for the poor, sweating Moroccan, the coup-de-grace was imminent. It was silent and swift. The old man turned and walked away down a tiny alley into his house and that was that. The Moroccan tried a few vain taps on doors and windows along the cobbled road, and proceeded on down the lane out to the main road.

Luigi rode in about half an hour later, and as we were loading the bike onto the car in the square, I noticed the poor, sweaty Moroccan man being picked up by a car driven by another Moroccan with two others already in the back. What a life, I thought. A chain of heists from boats and trucks out on the coast, then the boss, dishing out the goods to team captains and they in turn to these little bag men who probably make a subsistence, under-the-table living. Talking to the hawkers on the beach, we knew how it worked. Worst of all, they live perhaps twenty or so to a tiny rented apartment, throwing their sleeping bags out each night. Perhaps what they have come from is worse, who knows. As one man from Algeria told us, his whole family had been murdered by the insurgents and the trek across North Africa to Tangier to wait on the beach for three months for a boat to Italy was nothing in comparison to his life there.

❉ ❉ ❉

I had not really had any time the first week to wander round the villages to check on all my favorite people, so I was saddened to hear that Julia, the "Cat Lady's" old auntie, died early in the year. I am quite sure she is now happily helping Nona and all the other long-gone old ladies tend their higher gardens. Nona's roses were a mass of soft pink blooms this year and the red roses were climbing on the arbor. In fact the vines were now half way across and looking very verdant and healthy. The trees had grown enough to block most of the top road and I found myself feeling a bit sorry that I could no longer wave to Paolino on his tractor or the old ladies walking to church. As I thought about how my personality had changed, how I am now more sociable and would not mind at all if the villagers could see into our piazza, a smell of smoke caught my attention.

One of the fir trees on the lower side of the house was nicely singed on one side, thanks to Luigi's bonfire. As required, he had notified the town hall people that we would be burning garden wastes early in the morning. They then would ignore the smoke from the area. No one noticed until the next day when I mentioned that we had a lovely half-dead fir. Actually it was Eliza, the "Pizza Lady's" tree on the land that Nona had given her years before. "Wow," with huge innocent eyes, Luigi said. "Did I do that?" I mentioned that I had not seen anyone else running around with matches and gasoline and hosepipes. Later, he decided to burn the garden waste that we chuck over the wall down about fifteen feet onto Pierina's property, with her permission of course. She now has half a walnut tree and a streak of scorched field. Luigi's bonfire would not catch, so, not content with patience and a bit more paper and matches, my genius man produced a plastic bottle with a bit of gas in it, poured it on the pathetic, struggling fire, which immediately renewed. He then threw the empty bottle on. The biggest bang I have ever heard echoed across the valley as the "empty" bottle rocketed away down the hill leaving a trail of burned field in its wake. It reminded me of my father's fire making days, (my friends used to call him Uncle Bang, as he would light diesel bonfires just to annoy the neighbors, producing huge wooshing bangs). This time, all ended happily, the hosepipe in constant attention, the burn complete.

The burned fir tree stood on the piece of land on the south

east side of the house, overlooking the valley. With a crafty look, Luigi asked me if I would like to own that tree. I was surprised to say the least. Apparently Pepino next door had mentioned to him that he wanted to buy the piece of land, and had spoken to Eliza. The land was kitty-corner to his house, and was directly adjacent to our house so it made more sense that it belonged with No. 17 and not Pepino's house. The next day, Luigi negotiated a deal for us to buy the lot. Eliza had not been happy with Pepino's forceful approach, and asked Luigi not to tell anyone; she did not want to become involved in all the petty wrangling in Rovinaglia. Eliza was very accommodating and we made some satisfactory arrangements regarding payment. Funnily enough, the legal fees for transfer were more than the land was worth.

Trial by fire was certainly the order of the day as that evening, Luigi spotted a forest fire on the Tuscan ridge. None of the villagers would phone the Forestry Department but Luigi finally persuaded the "Dog Man" to phone. The crews were already, fortunately, on it, although it took ten hours to extinguish. Now we have two landslides, a rock pit, and acres of scorched hillside to enhance our glorious view!

Our experiences with fire were still not at an end. A strange happening was to occur which was as good as any of the stories told by the old people who gathered in the warm evenings to gossip. A couple of days before this particular fire, Luigi had been telling me how, during the war, he and his friend, their dads and two uncles were walking through the woods when they heard a group of German soldiers approaching. Being ardent Partisans, the men sought cover inside an old, huge Chestnut tree and sent the dog and the kids home. The men were, however, discovered and duly marched to the village and questioned. Harboring no secrets they were eventually released to their thankful families. This time good fortune was shining on them. I had never heard this story before, and so it was quite remarkable and eerily coincidental that two days later the tree still standing with its hollowed out trunk had burned to a charred shell. No other trees had burned. The field butting up to the tree line had five or six scorched spots joined by a long burned area about three feet wide, but nothing else was burned. The heroic old tree close to the edge of Genovese and which must have been eight feet in diameter was still smoking when I went to see it. I noticed that there were saplings growing from one smaller stump of the tree that had been sawed off sometime ago and one of the branches had survived, growing out of the only uncharred mossy green area on the trunk. So there is life in the old tree yet. The mystery is, how did it catch fire? We had had no recent lightening storms and none of the villagers would deliberately set a fire. Even the "bad kids" from the city would hardly be bothered to hike a mile across the fields to pick on one tree. So the mystery remains in the minds of the villagers. To be talked about, discussed, digested; to have as many different reasons for burning, as there were people discussing the event. I think it was an errant cigarette stub or perhaps a lightening strike that had smoldered for awhile before developing into a real fire. It was still puzzling in the fact that it did not spread!

After the "trials by fire" there was still much to do in preparation for the arrival of our son Carlo and his friend, who would be spending two weeks with us. The present plan of the house did not allow for much privacy, not that any of us cared, though their imminent arrival brought to the forefront a need for a door between the small bedroom for guests, and our bedroom. We remembered that Anna, Gloria's mother, had offered us the old shutters from Luigi's father, Lorenzo's house, which she had kept in the loft all these years. We thought of having the carpenter add a bottom to them, as we had done to Nona's old credenza windows, and with the louvered tops they would make very nice doors. Off we rushed to the carpenter and he said it would be a week. Perfect, we would have time to prepare the present opening to receive its lovely new doors. It was difficult trying to reason with

Luigi that we should not prepare the frame in the opening until we had the doors. Previous experience with the credenza doors, which still do not fit properly, remained fresh in my mind. I did not have enough fingers to count how many times the doors had been removed, the frame adjusted, and then replaced, however, this time I was successful.

The week before the doors were ready provided Luigi with ample time to invent the faux window. Never happy with the results of the rock wall in the kitchen, on which he had worked so hard to remove the old glass doors and good china cabinet, he decided despite his whining, negative, wife, to remove some rocks from the space that he had previously filled. He retrieved the louvered bottoms of the old shutters, which the carpenter was to replace with solid panels to form doors, and mounted them in the space. Wanting to make the least of what I considered to be a big mistake, I painted them white. I have to admit that his idea was a stroke of genius. Our faux window looks wonderful. I look forward to the day that Pierina pops in and opens up the faux windows to a beautiful view of the rock wall behind; it will afford us all a good giggle.

We picked up the doors for the small room two days before our visitors arrived. Woodworking is so easy in Canada,
two by fours, nails, screws, plywood, all in quick supply. Saw,
saw, bang, bang, and it is all done. Here we are dealing with
ancient rock walls, so it is much more the work of drilling
and cementing and things falling from between the beams
every time a hammer is wielded. The whole mouse's nest,
nicely lined with bits of my sheets, dropped out of the ceiling
once again, as we slaved for hours to finish the doors. I was
painting like mad while Luigi drove to Bologna to pick up
Carlo. They arrived back late in the evening, and sank bliss-
fully into a ten hour sleep, behind the lovely new doors.

Luigi and I wanted so much for them to see Pisa and
Florence, to visit nearby castles and markets, but two weeks

was not enough to see everything. Wanting to do their own thing they went away on the train to Milan and Florence to discover as much as they could in four days. Florence cast her wonderful spirit of enchantment and Milan helped to add to their stock of leather jackets and shoes. The marble mountains overlooking Carrara, the beach; and then Bardi castle and other local historical sites did the usual job of capturing hearts. As soon as they had arrived, it seemed it was time to leave, and off they flew to Canada loaded with the latest fashions in clothing and three kilos of parmesan.

✻ ✻ ✻

Ever since her first visit, my sister-in-law Annette, had begged my brother Christopher to come with her to visit No. 17. She knew he would just love the peace and solitude, thus our second group of visitors arrived the day after Carlo left. We took them to a couple of local historical sites but mostly they just wanted to sit in the sun and laze, overdosing on parmesan and cappuccino and wine! They tried several wines and one evening we chatted about our grandfather's ability to make fruit wines, and so the Elderberry wine was born. Christopher said, "Do you remember the elderberry wine that our grandfather used to make?"

"Of course I do," I said, "I remember our purple fingers after berry gathering expeditions." Every Monday morning after one of these expeditions, my teacher berated me for having stained fingers. Her shrill tight voice would shriek across the classroom, "This is not acceptable young lady." I would shrink in embarrassment as all eyes turned on me.

Christopher went to gather the elderberries, which grow profusely in this area, while I begged and borrowed some yeast and sugar and Annette and I cleaned and sterilized some old green bottles that Guilio gave me. Christopher returned with armloads of elderberries. Seen by Meri, she immediately came rushing round to Luigi screaming that some of them were poisonous. Some had red stalks, some black—but which was which? In the noise and mayhem and input from several other old folk it was impossible to determine. Now a bit red around the gills and still alive, my brother simply said "Oh, stuff it," and put the whole lot in the boiling water and stewed up a magnificent smelling brew. He and Annette then strained it through his new Italian socks, which he had to buy along with other basics as his travel bag had gone off to Timbucktoo instead of Parma. Duly bottled and cooled we discussed who might be the first guinea pig. I offered figuring it could only kill or cure me but was voted down. Luigi and Annette would not dare so it was left to my brother. He woofed up half a glass, said it was great and having not dropped dead in thirty seconds, had another glass. As he remained standing, I also had a glass. It was very good. We stored a few bottles in the cantina and have not heard yet that a purple bomb has gone off at No. 17.

Staying only a week their holiday came to a quick end. Popping them on the train for Parma, we returned to the house to shut it down for another year as we were leaving the following day. A magic moment occurred when Mussi arrived at the door with the land titles finalized. Signed, sealed and delivered; never was an aphorism truer. Now we had our beautiful pieces of land, our own mushrooms, chestnuts, woodcutting places, and the adjacent piece of land from Eliza. We would not have to tear down the arbor as the "Land Baron" had predicted. We would not have our view destroyed by Pepino building on that lot, another idea created, fed and watered by the "Land Baron". This little unassuming house now proudly sat on the hillside, our very own piece of Emilia. She had floated in limbo for so long but now was anchored forever.

A little bit of icing on the cake was Christopher's phone call with news that our special rock might indeed be Roman. He had taken a photograph of the rock and shown it to an archeologist in London. We hoped this might be true, but even if not we still had a wonderful historical monument set in the wall of the house.

All the usual chores performed — mothballing, winterizing pipes, turning off electricity, were a mixture of sadness but at the same time great joy. I watched Luigi taking care of some last minute deeds, and left a note taped to the kitchen door asking that those who might enter should ensure the cats did not get locked inside.

Leaving this year was a landmark occasion for us. Since 1996, we had struggled to obtain legal ownership of No. 17, and land in close proximity. At last, success! It was a good feeling, closing up our very own house and saying goodbye to our very own piece of Italy. A tiny, but precious piece of my beloved Emilia, forever in my heart, perpetuating my love affair with this beautiful part of Italy.

Oh Emilia, my heart aches as we drive away, but as I turn for one last look, my eye catches a glint of sun from the dear little mail box now mounted proudly on the wall of No. 17, announcing the names of the owners, Luigi Ferrari and Virginia Gabriella Colbourne!

ISBN 141202780-2

9 781412 027809